Tom Vowler is an award-winning novelist and short story writer living in south-west England. His debut collection, *The Method*, won the Scott Prize in 2010 and the Edge Hill Readers' Prize in 2011, while his novels, *What Lies Within* and *That Dark Remembered Day*, received critical acclaim. He is editor of the literary journal *Short Fiction* and an associate lecturer in creative writing at Plymouth University, where he completed his PhD.

www.tomvowler.co.uk
@tom_vowler

The Method

What Lies Within

That Dark Remembered Day

DAZZLING THE GODS

— Stories —

Tom Vowler

Unbound

This edition first published in 2018

Unbound
6th Floor Mutual House, 70 Conduit Street, London W1S 2GF
www.unbound.com

© Tom Vowler, 2018

Epigraph quotation from *A Monster Calls* by Patrick Ness, based on an original idea by Siobhan Dowd, © 2C   ondon SE11 5HJ.

LONDON BOROUGH OF WANDSWORTH	
9030 00005 8728 0	
Askews & Holts	01-Feb-2018
AF	£8.99
	WW17019393

'Debt' won t   f their anthology. A version of   e Twice Drowned Woman'. 'At   *nal*. 'Dazzling the Gods' was fe   published online in the *Wales*   Story Prize 2016. 'The Offspri   ara' was first published in Issue 17 of *Prole* magazine, 'Fireflies' in *The Simple Things* magazine. 'The Grandmaster of Gaza' first appeared in Issue 3 of *The Lonely Crowd*, and later in *Two Thirds North*. 'Blowhole' appeared in *Unthology 10*. 'An Arrangement' was published in Issue 3 of *Banshee*. 'Lucca: Last Days of a Marriage' appeared in Issue 6 of *The Lonely Crowd*. My thanks to the editors of these journals.

While every effort has been made to trace the owners of copyright material reproduced herein, the publisher would like to apologise for any omissions and will be pleased to incorporate missing acknowledgements in any further editions.

Text Design by Ellipsis

A CIP record for this book is available from the British Library.

ISBN 978-1-78352-399-3 (trade pbk)
ISBN 978-1-78352-400-6 (ebook)
ISBN 978-1-78352-398-6 (limited edition)

Printed in Great Britain by Clays Ltd, St Ives Plc

1 3 5 7 9 8 6 4 2

MIX
Paper from
responsible sources
FSC® C018179

Stories are the wildest things of all, the monster rumbled.
Stories chase and bite and hunt.

Patrick Ness, *A Monster Calls*

Dear Reader,

The book you are holding came about in a rather different way to most others. It was funded directly by readers through a new website: Unbound. Unbound is the creation of three writers. We started the company because we believed there had to be a better deal for both writers and readers. On the Unbound website, authors share the ideas for the books they want to write directly with readers. If enough of you support the book by pledging for it in advance, we produce a beautifully bound special subscribers' edition and distribute a regular edition and ebook wherever books are sold, in shops and online.

This new way of publishing is actually a very old idea (Samuel Johnson funded his dictionary this way). We're just using the internet to build each writer a network of patrons. At the back of this book, you'll find the names of all the people who made it happen.

Publishing in this way means readers are no longer just passive consumers of the books they buy, and authors are free to write the books they really want. They get a much fairer return too – half the profits their books generate, rather than a tiny percentage of the cover price.

If you're not yet a subscriber, we hope that you'll want to join our publishing revolution and have your name listed in one of our books in the future. To get you started, here is a £5 discount on your first pledge. Just visit unbound.com, make your pledge and type **dazzle5** in the promo code box when you check out.

Thank you for your support,

Dan, Justin and John
Founders, Unbound

CONTENTS

Debt

I pick him up from the airport. My younger brother, home under the cover of night to make good everything again.

'You look all skinny,' he says. 'Jane not feeding you?'

As we release each other, I offer to take his bag but he ignores me.

'I lucked out with the cabin crew,' he says. 'They used to be up for a bit of flirting; came with the job.'

I picture my brother attaching himself limpet-like to some jet-lagged woman, who in a bar or at a party would extract herself with a weary refrain, but who, at 28,000 feet, has no enduring escape routes.

'Don't you ever have a day off?' I say.

'The world is what it is, little brother.' Despite the year and a bit I have on him, he's called me this since bulking out in his late teens. 'You should come over and stay,' he says. 'Taste some Mediterranean delights.'

Over was in the hills outside Marbella, Conor's home for the last four years, chosen when run-ins with Dublin's petty criminals progressed to something potentially mortal. There had been no time for goodbyes, our mother phoning me in a panic when she realised he'd left in the small hours one New Year's Eve.

I'd long since moved out – another kind of fleeing, I suppose – a vestige of respectability found teaching music at a failing Galway comprehensive. Far enough away to visit if I had to, but with an infrequency that suited me. My departure meant our sister was now the sole provider of nurturance to a mother who measured the day's passing in alcoholic rather than temporal units. Our father, not much good at life either, at least had the sense to get out before his own tyranny imprisoned him, leaving the day before my 15th birthday. Our mother's judgement was typically understated. 'You'll all leave in the end,' she said.

'Maybe I'll come over in the holidays,' I say.

'Bring some crisps with you; they have no idea about crisps.'

Conor lights a cigarette, opens the car window a crack. He smells of something I can't place, the odour of a foreign life. A good life, I imagine, though I know nothing of its particulars.

'Things working out for you over there?' I say.

'Ah, you know, sun, sea and all that shite. I play golf every morning. Can you believe it? I used to hate those pricks with their polo shirts and their buggies. Now I'm one of them.'

'You're right, I don't believe it.'

'No good, though. I hook everything. Grip's too strong, apparently.'

I imagine the club in his hands, absent of all finesse.

'You got work?' I say.

'When I want it.'

'Legal?'

'Hey, come on. I've been back five minutes. What is this?'

'I'm interested, that's all.'

He turns the radio on, scans through the stations, settling on some whiny rock anthem that sees him drum the dashboard, which should annoy me but somehow doesn't. The road south is quiet at this time of night, allowing me to watch a chalky moon sat large over the city. I think to say I'm happy he's back, how it's good to see him, but just drive instead.

'You had this long?' Conor says, making a play of checking the seatbelt.

'Couple of years.'

'And you haven't written it off yet? I'm impressed.'

'Funny.'

The last time I saw my brother his foot had a man's head fixed to the floor. I'd come home for the holidays and he'd taken me on a tour of his latest nocturnal haunts – disagreeable places in the north of Dublin – and I soon got the sense it was for my benefit, his illegitimate world proudly paraded, as if to make the point his was a successful life despite the absence of an honest vocation. As one by one he introduced me to men I sensed were best avoided, I imagined the inverse: of my showing him round the school, meeting colleagues in the staffroom, eating in the canteen. Midway through the evening an argument broke out in a nightclub, an acquaintance of Conor's unable to appease a group of disgruntled customers, my brother approaching with quiet relish as he took out the most vocal of them. Go in quick and hard, his way. For weeks, whenever the Head annoyed me, I imagined employing such decisive conflict resolution. I remember before our father left, he told me he'd never have to worry about Conor, that he would always be able to look after himself, the implication being that I couldn't.

Absent of an obvious authority figure, Conor's passage through adolescence became progressively turbulent, although when I left for the west coast, his criminal record remained modest, boasting little more than vandalism, a caution for shoplifting and possession of some Class B. Charm and good fortune, as much as his physique, seemed to insulate him from the more extreme elements of retribution his lifestyle yielded. Until, that was, the wrong people were crossed, liberties taken where none were tolerated. According to our sister, he lost several kilograms of Colombia's finest in a bungled deal, the money handed over before he'd collected the gear. It was enough that an example needed making.

*

The house is cold when we get back. At the top of the stairs light bleeds beneath our mother's bedroom door.

'I'll say hello,' Conor says.

'Leave her, it's late. She's probably fallen asleep reading.' I tell him our sister will be over tomorrow, if she can get off work.

'Does she know why I'm here?'

I nod. He seems indifferent to this. We hadn't involved her, other than my telling her I'd sort things, to not worry. Going to our brother wouldn't have been her approach, but families like ours can hardly go to the Garda.

I search the cupboards. Mum's stash is significant but low on variety. I pour us each some cheap-looking vodka, ask Conor if he wants ice, but he just takes the glass from me.

I first heard of Davy Coughlan before moving away, a small-time loan shark operating out of the next estate. Neighbours sometimes used him in the run-up to Christmas, weekly repayments made on the doorstep, an informal yet binding arrangement. According to our sister, Coughlan's empire had grown as hard times returned, buying up the debts of several other illegal lenders, his reach spreading south down to Navan Road and beyond. He had several full-time collectors, men and women who squeezed what they could from you, latitude given if you promised to pay double the next week. And when you couldn't, someone more persuasive would call round, the tone shifting from community redeemer to something more menacing. Despite her alcoholism, our mother, as far

7

as we knew, had always handled financial affairs ably, our father's absence focusing her mind on surviving alone with three children and a modest, unreliable income. And while we went without plenty, she managed to create the illusion that we weren't poor, fashioning free entertainment where possible, cheating the social out of a few quid. Since securing a half-decent job, I offered to send her money but it was always refused. Nobody knew for sure when she began using Coughlan, sometime after the last of us moved out, our sister thought.

'It was just enough to tide her over till her cheque came through,' Sheenah had told me on the phone last week. 'Like getting stuff from the catalogue, paying it back here and there.'

'How much?'

'She'd never say, told me not to worry.'

'So you didn't?'

'I don't think you get to be critical anymore.'

'But she was paying it off?'

'She almost had, but Coughlan's goons convinced her to borrow more, to pay off the last of the first loan and have some left over, and it carried on like this. I did a rough calculation of the interest rate, it's crazy. Last week someone came round, started asking who owned the house, took some jewellery as collateral.'

Conor pours us another drink, large ones. Despite the circumstances of our reunion, it's a relief to escape, for now, the path my own shortcomings are tempting me along. For the best part of a term I've ignored the unambiguous attentions of a pupil in my A-level class, dismissing the thoughts as they gather in my mind, telling myself such crushes were a vocational inevitability, that they pass with time. A promising cellist, the girl's compositional techniques were far advanced of her peers, and although I liked to encourage the creation of ensemble pieces, she excelled as a solo performer, the sublimity of her music the contrast of these shitty streets I grew up in. And for now I've behaved with professionalism, the line in my mind clear and precise, the problems with my marriage never exploited. I imagine Conor faced with a similar situation, regarding its glorious potential, life holding such simplicity for his kind, the devoted servant of hedonism, of base needs.

My brother downs his drink. As his shirt rises I glimpse a heavily tattooed arm and remember the ones we gave each other as kids, crosses clumsily scrawled on our biceps, my own now weathered to an indistinct blue-green blemish. We pierced each other's ears too, a bloody affair, Conor's becoming infected, though he stuck with it, sporting to this day a silver ring. Other memories return unbidden. Of escaping the city's clutches, walking for miles, climbing trees to add to our collection of birds' eggs, a cache that presumably still lies in the loft here.

We started a fire once, in a barn we'd broken into, watching from a distant hill as the flames grew, feeling perhaps it had gone too far. Or just that it was something to regret, the wanton destruction of someone's property, an act other kids would have regarded frivolous, but that left us sombre for a day or two.

He asks about Mum, berates me for not visiting more.

'Work's busy just now.'

'She needs looking after.'

'Perhaps we should all come and live with you, play golf every day.'

'With your fair skin? You'd last a week.'

'I'll bring a hat.'

I tell him more about Coughlan, stuff our sister had said.

'Right,' he says, 'we do this tomorrow night.'

'I've been thinking we should just pay it off. I've got some savings.'

'You can wait in the car if you like. I'll go in on my own.'

'You want me to come?'

'Someone has to drive. Come on, you're good at that these days.'

I want to say how absurd this all is, now that it's real. That I have a good job, more than that, I have a career to think of. There should be a more rational response to consider.

'Anyway,' he says, 'why call me if you've doubts?'

Because I knew you'd come back. Because I miss

having you around. Because you just left, my younger yet somehow older brother.

'I don't know,' I say.

Conor tops us up once more.

'Your car reliable?' he asks, and I nod. 'Good. Tomorrow, then. Best get some kip.'

I gesture towards the spare room, offer to take the sofa.

'I'm fine on there,' he says. 'You take the bed.'

The next day we leave a few hours after dark. What sleep I'd managed was fitful, occupied by the formless spectres of fear, Conor's snoring a comfort on waking. Earlier our mother had cooked for the four of us, the food from another generation but surprisingly agreeable. She seemed unconcerned by my brother's sudden presence, delighting in the rare convergence of all her children. Our sister, too, imparted none of her usual animosity at our enduring absence.

After dinner Conor made some calls, presumably to get an address, perhaps to say hello to old friends. We'd searched the house and shed for something of Dad's, an old hurling stick or cricket bat, settling for a small crowbar from the garage. And then we go, across town, streets slicked with rain, lamps jaundicing the way. Conor's cigarette fills the car with a piquant fug, evoking some long forgotten aspect of our father, who would sit smoking for hours at the dining table, gazing at the window, perhaps planning his exodus.

My brother was disciplined, as our father termed it, most weeks, sometimes following a letter from school highlighting his absence or some misdemeanour. Or he'd come in late, dinner missed, clothes torn from a fight, his punishment rarely administered in the sobriety of the moment, reserved instead for a Friday night once the pub had closed, when the house was still and I'd listen to Conor's muffled cries through my bedroom wall.

Our father never struck me, though; it was as if my brother soaked up all his violent reserves. Around the time we set fire to the barn, I'd begun messing about in the garage, sitting in the Cortina listening to a tape, easing the gearstick back and forth, imagining some girl next to me, wind in her hair, the promise of lustful delights. One day, for reasons I can't recall, our father walked the two miles to work and on returning from school I found the car keys hanging in the hallway, figuring that a single lap of the garage block would go unnoticed. Unable to adjust the seat, I could barely reach the pedals, yet went ahead anyway, seduced by the engine's roar, by the drama of the thing.

The damage was minimal but impossible to miss, our father certain to discover it the following day. Later I showed Conor, who laughed an unconvincing laugh as we crouched together in the garage, inspecting the outcome of my misadventure.

'He loves this car,' was all my brother said.

Dinner that evening was the usual quiet affair, Sheenah pushing vegetables from one side of her plate to the other, our mother lost to thoughts of some other life she might have led. I could hardly eat for fear, an image of the dented and scratched wing vivid in my mind. Out looking for nests once, Conor had spoken of the belt our father used, thick and ridged, its swift movement leaving the air charged.

How many times? I'd asked, both wanting and not wanting to know. To get through it, Conor told me he imagined me standing behind our father, carrying out the same sentence on him, blow by blow.

When my brother spoke at dinner that night, it was almost with nonchalance, the act of lying coming easily to him by then, as he described how his foot had slipped on the pedal, how he tried to brake in time, the sound of metal on brick. How he would save his pocket money and pay for the repairs. Our father listened to the confession in silence, before heading out to the garage, where he stayed until it got dark.

As always the reckoning came days later, the whole house seeming to resound with the violence, our father going too far this time, even for him. And perhaps he feared he'd kill my brother one day, as the world seemed reordered after that night. Either way, he left a week later.

*

Conor asks about the car, what it does to the gallon. He seems relaxed, as if we're visiting family or heading for a night out, remarking on all the changes to this part of town.

'Ever thought of coming back?' I say.

'Not really.'

'Perhaps it's all been forgotten.'

'These people don't forget. Anyway, come back for what?'

'You could head my way. No one knows you there.'

'Do you know how much rain southern Spain gets?'

'Fair enough.'

Conor flicks his cigarette out the window, tells me to take a left up ahead.

'You all settled down with Jane now?' he says.

'I guess.'

'Don't it scare you, the same woman for the rest of your life?'

'Why should it?'

'No variety, never fucking someone for the first time again.'

'There's more than fucking.'

He laughs, as if I couldn't possibly believe this, and for a moment, after all these years, I almost ask him why he lied for me. Instead I say, 'Do you ever wonder where he went? What he's doing?'

'No, not really.'

*

I wait in the car, apparently to keep watch but effectively redundant, a provider of transport, hands and conscience clean, eyes witness to nothing more than the initial orchestration. I wonder how often my brother does something like this these days, whether there are others in his adopted country who take care of such matters for him now.

'Some people only understand one way, one language,' he'd said last night.

'And if it makes things worse for her?'

'I'll come back.'

A young couple, a little drunk, sidle along the pavement, the man stumbling into the wing mirror, knocking it askew, the woman apologising before laughing. I try to hunker down, feign indifference, but the man – a boy really, I see now – feels the need to make a point, his face an inch from the windscreen, breath misting the glass as he studies me. You need to go, I want to say. You need to go before my brother returns and things go badly for you. The girl pulls his coat, pleads with him, a hint in her voice of being witness to such events too often. My giving him nothing to feed off eventually works and after a final flourish of menace he allows the girl to lead him away, down the road, the boy howling into the night like some demented creature.

I stare at the building across the road, the door Conor entered with the crowbar, trying to calculate how long it's been, how many men Coughlan might have up there. I'd made him promise just to issue a warning, his visit a symbol of our resistance, that we, that our mother, wouldn't simply roll over and pay up.

It occurs to me that we should have parked further away, that bringing the car here in an age of ubiquitous CCTV was foolish. I consider how frightened by everything I am – being here now, the aggression of a passing boy, the guilt of an imagined affair – all of it taking me back to the dinner table that night, to the disciplining Conor saved me from.

Had I always been a coward? So innately weak that even our father was reluctant to expose it, made as I am of different stuff? Perhaps Conor is on some level thankful for the man's brutish hand, it hardening him, forging him like a blacksmith's hammer, preparing him for the world he would know.

Stepping out of the car I can smell my childhood, a thousand memories assembling at the promise of their indulgence. I picture Jane reading in our bed, my safe and comfortable life so removed from this place, yet the link never entirely severed. I imagine my class on Monday, the ruinous thoughts that will line up in attack formation. How I'll do the right thing and be resentful for it. I consider my sister's face, how something in her eyes resembles utterly my own, our complexions alike – ashen, almost ethereal – Conor's swarthy by comparison, even before his expatriation, marking him out for our father's attention from the start.

Unsolicited, a mealtime routine of sorts comes to mind, a rare glimpse of another side to our father, who whenever my brother asked if he could get down from the table, would reply, 'No, son, you can only get down from a duck.' He said it in response without fail, the two of them trading guarded smiles as if it was the first time.

Perhaps I will go to visit him, get away from it all for a while, arrive with every flavour of crisp. Jane might come, the trip a new start, the sun nourishing us. I picture us finding Conor on the tee, his grip loosened a little as the club scythes downward, connecting cleanly, the ball cutting without deviation through crystalline Spanish sky, mile after mile.

The city is quieter now, burnished in moonlight. Ignoring my heart's frequent, heavy beat I open the door across the street, negotiate the stairs in near-darkness, almost tripping as I run to find my brother.

At the Musée D'Orsay

They made their way, all four of them, through the glass awning and into the cavernous belly of the museum, its lavishly carved stone walls rising to a barrel-vaulted glass ceiling. He watched as Brett and Lottie ploughed through the crowd, leaving him and Sally to offer apologetic smiles in their wake. Earlier, in a rare moment of privacy, when the two couples were separated crossing Pont Neuf, his wife agreed they'd outgrown their once-friends, how visiting had been a mistake, but that it was prudent to make the most of the stay, neither having visited Paris beyond a school trip or to make a connecting train.

The two women had met a dozen or so years ago at art college, losing touch briefly when Lottie took a job at the National Gallery, where a few months later she happened upon Brett, a hedge fund manager turned art dealer from one of the smaller Channel Islands. When Sally was offered a teaching post in the South Downs, their relocation saw the emergence of regular social encounters between the four, scores of dinner parties he tolerated for his wife's sake. Brett immediately struck him as the sort who yearned for times an Englishman could keep a snow leopard as a pet, or could flounce around the globe drawing deference rather than contempt. The man made no concession to small talk, which seemed to pain him, and did little to hide his boredom when others spoke. Despite this they were able to occupy conversational ground that offended neither, riding the contrails of whatever topic the women initiated. Occasionally, when the two were left alone, Brett would offer him supposedly privileged advice on investments, which he politely observed, though in truth there was rarely anything left at the end of the month for such speculation.

'Get on board early with this one,' Brett would say conspiratorially, as if they were discussing an affair one of them was having. 'Just don't sit on them forever.'

His own job, interviewing candidates for social housing, was often rewarding, but presumably its remuneration belonged to another realm entirely. It also left him feeling inferior whenever art, fine or otherwise, was discussed. Sally, however, clearly regarded the friendship worthy of prolonging, citing the importance of keeping company with more than one manner of person.

The matter, though, was taken out of their hands when Brett and Lottie, appalled by the prospect of, as they termed it, another socialist government, had a year ago exchanged a flat just off the Thames for a luxury apartment overlooking the Seine. Occupying the third and fourth floors of an historic building on Quai Henri IV, the property, reached by a gilded elevator, had been decadently renovated, its showpiece a wrap-around balcony over-looking the city. The furniture was antique, the art exclusive.

'Eleven hundred square feet,' Brett had said when they arrived, as if he'd counted all of them. There was air conditioning for each of the seven rooms and a security system to embarrass a head of state.

After unpacking, Sally had asked if they might take a boat trip.

'Don't be silly, Sal,' said Lottie. 'Those are for the tourists.'

By way of compromise they observed the Catacombs at Montparnasse before hanging out in the boutiques and bars of Rue Oberkampf, allowing their hosts to drizzle proceedings with what smattering of French they'd bothered to learn. Later Lottie bought Italian ravioli and a large wedge of Comté from the fragrant stalls of the Marché des Enfants Rouge, using the latter for a fondue that evening. The dinner, although overly rich, was pleasant enough, and once he'd resigned to taking a minor role in exchanges, it seemed a certain enjoyment might even be had.

The following day, after coffee and croissants on the sun-kissed balcony, they had cocktails in the Hemingway Bar at the Ritz, before spending a boozy afternoon sampling Burgundies and Pinot Noirs in a nearby *caviste*, where Brett spoke endlessly of *terroir* and his dislike for New World reds. Later, after their hosts argued and Brett followed a tearful Lottie back to the apartment, he and Sally took a cruise down the Seine with the other tourists.

The crowd in the museum had thinned now, their hosts suggesting they have a drink as it was still early, the four of them taking the stairs and then the escalator to the brasserie on the fifth floor. They had been due to attend the ballet that evening – Brett having complimentary tickets for *La Sylphide* – but a phone call to the apartment after lunch elicited in him a state of barely contained excitement. If they didn't mind foregoing the ballet, a marvellous opportunity had presented itself. A show – one-off and strictly invitation only – was to be held in a private room of the Musée d'Orsay after closing hours.

'What sort of show?' he had asked Brett.

'Nothing you'd see at home. This guy is going to be huge. He's pushing all the boundaries of performance art.'

'No one really knows who he is,' said Lottie. 'Viennese they think. Oh, please say you'll come.'

They found a table beneath a majestic, outward-facing clock, a relic, according to Brett, from when the building had been a railway station. Beginning to feel lethargic from all the excess, he ordered an espresso, picturing himself climbing the chalk hills of home, watching the sun slip behind Linch Down, not a gallery or bar in sight. Did people here live like this all the time, flitting from one cultural gorging to another, or had they been subjected to a particularly rarefied tour, a condensed version reserved for impressionable guests? He wasn't ungrateful for such hospitality; he just couldn't keep up any more.

Brett was speaking of England.

'Country's gone to the dogs. We should have moved years ago. You guys should come over, buy somewhere.' By somewhere, presumably he meant a cupboard in the suburbs.

'We'd miss Sussex too much,' said Sally.

'Yes, I expect you would.'

There was something in Brett's eyes now, perhaps the anticipation of whatever spectacle they were about to witness, or just an air of superiority – a look that reminded him of the stag weekend he'd been obliged to attend after Sally and Lottie resumed their friendship. At the behest of Brett's best man, they'd convened, half a dozen of them, at a cottage on the edge of the New Forest, the others, he assumed, fellow denizens of the Square Mile. Within an hour of his arriving they accounted for a bottle of Jura and several lines of cocaine, some future version of himself no doubt appalled but helpless to intervene. By way of preparation, he'd vowed the only way to get through the occasion was to indulge whatever forms of destruction were on offer, while promising Sally he'd do his best to return unscathed. Being resident in the countryside, he reasoned, would at least ensure their non-attendance at some lap dancing lair or worse. Instead, much of the weekend was spent in sporting combat – archery, racquetball, a little golf – which considering how much they drank was to be commended. He fared badly at most, yet didn't disgrace himself. The *pièce de résistance*, though, was held back until the Sunday evening, just as he was thinking no more could be endured. A landowner had been paid some obscene amount to permit a few acres of woodland be given over for a nocturnal paintball melee, last man standing and all that. There followed some of the worst hours of his life, as they spent half the night stalking each other in the rain, every now and then discharging spheres of fluorescent paint at a shifting shadow or ambient noise. Only later did he discover Brett and the others had night vision scopes on their weapons, leaving him exposed to the tyranny of several drunk and high feral bankers.

They were deep in the bowels of the building now, Lottie giggling like a child as Brett led the way through labyrinthine corridors. He'd told them earlier there would be no time to see any Degas or Gauguin, as Sally had requested, that tonight was all about the future of art. Finally they reached a door, in front of which a security guard stood impassively. Perhaps the man knew Brett, as he asked in English for them to relinquish their phones, which could, he said, be collected from reception after the show. The guard then scanned them with a handheld device, before allowing them to enter.

The room itself was dimly lit, its far corners beyond sight. They were shown by a young woman to a row of seats that arced in a semicircle, perhaps a couple of dozen people sitting in front and behind them, the silence broken only by an occasional cough or the door they'd entered through opening and closing.

Dating Sally in their student days he'd attended many such events, supposedly audacious exhibitions and performances, designed to shock or outrage, but which more often than not he found passé or inane. Perhaps, in one way or another, everything had been said or done, originality beyond even the most subversive of intentions. Maybe art needed a clean start, a new race of post-apocalyptic cave dwellers, unburdened by the weight of history as they daubed the rock in charcoal. Or would precisely the same masterpieces evolve all over again, humans incapable of escaping their aesthetic destiny?

It was a couple of miles to the apartment but they agreed the evening air would be welcome, a chance to reflect on what they'd just witnessed, and so they walked along Quai de Conti, past Notre-Dame, its stonework ochreous against the gloaming Parisian sky. He was thankful Brett and Lottie went on ahead, the orange glow from Brett's cigarette cutting a hole in the night as he gesticulated like a native.

Of course none of it was real, despite the artist's assurances to that effect. And yet it was beyond his imagination how the ghastly trick was achieved. He presumed the fainting woman in front of them to be a stooge; as too the few who left mid-act, tearful or appalled. Or perhaps they were just credulous; certainly no one around them seemed to share his scepticism.

The artist – if that was the correct term – had finally appeared through a pair of black curtains at the front of the room. Dressed in dark trousers and polo neck, he looked around 40, though was clearly younger, his eyes intense, almost pained, his face a series of sharp angles, as if the skin was being drawn from within. Physically there was nothing to him, his willowy frame rising to an ovate head, the goatee beard at its base quite satanic. His complexion was of someone who lived entirely indoors, or who had mere hours to live, yet when he spoke, his voice boomed among them without need of amplification, its timbre pealing like a church bell. There followed a rather arcane rant – the screen behind the man translating his words into several languages – the gist of which was an antipathy towards bourgeois art lovers, in particular critics who possessed no talent themselves. But instead of alienating the audience, this seemed merely to rouse their fascination, as murmurs of approval stole across the room. Apparently, few understood what true artists went through, the sacrifices that were made, least not those who sought to own their work, to own *them*. Yet this artist's work, the man said, would never be owned.

The screen was then filled with the words *ars longa,*

vita brevis, while what might have been Wagner started up around them. An older woman, similarly dressed and with close-cropped black hair, wheeled in a small trolley, on which sat a cream ceramic bowl and a metallic tray of surgical instruments. The artist quietly acknowledged her and placed his hands in the water, drying them on a towel she passed him. At the same time the woman who'd shown them to their seats pushed a wheelchair into the room, in which sat a barely conscious middle-aged man, a sign around his neck bearing the words '*un critique*'.

It was difficult to say how long what happened next took. Perhaps some sort of mass hypnosis had occurred, the screen laced with subliminal tidings, though all they'd seen was an endless loop of the critic's scathing reviews, hatchet jobs that took delight in the denigration of various artists. It was, they were told, his forte.

He supposed concentrating on the critic's eyes had been the ultimate symbolic gesture, the artist literally removing the man's ability to appreciate art again. Ensuring the act's detail went unmissed, especially by those seated further back, a close-up appeared on the screen, as the scalpel blade was carefully introduced to one eyeball and then the other. And with Wagner almost drowning out the critic's screams, the young woman returned, offering the artist a small liquid-filled container, in which he placed his pair of trophies.

*

As they walked he tried to take Sally's hand but she was still lost to shock, her shuffle along the quayside burdened with a sight that could not be unseen. As much as anything, it was their taking part, their willingness to vote for what happened, to determine the critic's fate. A descent, albeit fugacious, into savagery.

'You know it wasn't real?' he told her again. 'It was a performance.'

'But the blood . . .'

They continued on in silence for a few minutes, finally catching up with the others, who'd stopped for a drink outside a small bar. By now the Seine was ablaze with great whorls of impressionistic light, as if Van Gogh himself had been busy in their absence. As he shepherded Sally into her seat, a smug-looking Brett poured them some wine while Lottie bemoaned their having to leave in the morning.

'It feels like you've just got here,' she said. 'There's so much more to see.'

Dazzling the Gods

Even the bluebottles have succumbed. Half a dozen, upended on the window sill, legs sculling the air in attempts to right themselves. The room a kiln, sun furious as it seethes onto the glass, braising him in a broth of wretchedness. People comparing it to a time before all this, when there were standpipes in the road and you could cook an egg on the kerb.

Sitting up in bed he eyes the net curtain for hints of a breeze, some portent today will be cooler. Their sheets reek again, despite his having washed them yesterday, and he unfurls them from the window where they hang in limp surrender. In the kitchen he fills a glass with ice and water.

Electra left the flat before he woke; hopefully the heat or a need for food drove her out so early, and not another capitulation. As far as he knows she's been clean for a month; still some way short of his own effort, but a start all the same. He'd stuck with her each time she caved in to the tyranny of cravings, every setback hardening his resolve. Strangely, he found withdrawal, if not easy, then manageable once those first hellish days were negotiated, although he knows such dependence reaches into the marrow and never entirely recedes.

Looking around he estimates a single carload will do: clothes, scores of tools, a bureau that had been his grand-father's. Where uncertainty exists over ownership, or they acquired something together, he will leave it behind, an act born of guilt or kindness, he is unsure. Her absence this morning has given him the option of cowardice, his farewell scrawled rather than spoken. The kind of letter you write when the mix becomes one part love, two parts loathing. Perhaps she already senses his departure and has chosen not to witness it, preferring a silent cleaving.

He downs the water, rolls the glass across his forehead. Already the floor pulses to the music below, incessant bass that will reach deep into the weekend. He turns the radio on, a politician and scientist blaming each other, arguing about the figures, the tipping point. Outside the city groans and withers and looks skyward for relief.

She struck him last night. Something between a slap and a punch to the side of the head.

'It's the heat,' she said later, stroking the mark to his face. 'We need to get out of this place.'

Even then, despite what the drug had taken from her, he thought her beautiful, hoped some essence of it might be salvaged, nightfall affording sufficient respite. But when sleep came it brought only images of the baby.

*

He thinks about washing up last night's plates. It's an exaggeration to term the flat squalid, but it has long ceased being homely, their upkeep sufficient only for a life of sorts. After getting clean he found work at a scrapyard, welding skips four days a week, cash in hand. The men there, perhaps mindful of a rapid turnover, keep to themselves, sharing nothing but muted cigarette breaks with him. The only ones to converse are the Romanians, eager to practise newly-learnt phrases on him or to discuss the politics of their country. From what he understands, more than anything they miss a food called *sarmale*, a type of stuffed cabbage best enjoyed with smoked meat and sour cream. That and *țuică*, a strong spirit made from plums and sold in markets or by the roadside in unmarked bottles. The youngest showed him a family photo once, wife and newborn, told him he was welcome to visit anytime he was in Eastern Europe. When your own country is underwater, he half joked.

Since the latest heatwave, the owner of the yard allows them to start at 5am – it's bad for business having workers die – and they finish around midday, whereupon he comes home and collapses half-dead in a cold shower, his body brutalised yet purged some more. Electra would still be in bed, her logic that shorter days narrow temptation's window. When she did get up, a frisson of energy flashed through her and she'd reel off extravagant plans for their escape, to live in the country, clean and healthy, to start over. They would keep hens, make ginger beer.

'Everyone should be able to see the horizon,' she liked to say. 'Everyone should hear birdsong.'

Such manic bouts burned themselves out by evening, replaced with uneasy silence, with sleepless nights where she'd wail and thrash and spit and blame him for their purgatory. It was true he introduced her to heroin, a week or so after they met, when smoking it had been enough.

'It'll be OK,' he'd whisper, trying to hold her, and she'd tell him to say something that wasn't a lie.

In the beginning, when their bodies took hungrily from each other, her tongue hot in his mouth, his dreams laced with her, it never occurred to him to keep something back, to shore up that part of the self too brittle to expose.

He watches the cars below snarl and stammer nowhere, white light blazing off their roofs, dazzling the gods. Sirens start up to the south, like dogs prompting one another. Last week the young Romanian was sent home with suspected retina burn, a weld flash from someone's gun as he removed his helmet prematurely. They knew not to go to the hospital, but to bathe the eyes in milk or use a saline solution until someone came round, a doctor of sorts. Two days off, they were allowed, unpaid, and if a fuss was made, someone else, not a doctor of sorts, came round. The pain, he knew from his days as an apprentice, would arrive in the night, like hot sand rubbed hard into the cornea. You might as well stare at the sun.

He makes a strong coffee and listens to the couple

next door argue. The side of his face still smarts a little, a hotness overlying the ambient heat. He never retaliated, hadn't even raised his voice when she continued using. It was the perfect reason to stop, of course, for only the most selfish and cruel junkie continued poisoning a body that encased another.

He rolls a cigarette, listens to the soft sizzle as he draws on it. There'll be financial contrails to his leaving, some of which he hopes the envelope of cash will remedy. He'll pay the rent for a month or two, until she sorts something.

He fills a couple of bin sacks with clothes, sweating with the exertion. At the back of a drawer he finds a toddler's bodysuit, neatly folded with tags intact. A gift from a neighbour, it escaped Electra's cull when, unable to give everything up, he'd hidden it there. He brings the fabric to his face, inhales its scent, but it's just his own. He'll visit the hospital later. There's a memorial garden in the grounds, an entire plot devoted to the premature, where they'd taken flowers a couple of times soon after and again on the anniversary, until even this lapsed to neglect.

When you befriend heroin, you begin a slow and steady walk towards a rotating buzz saw. Whether or not you can deviate from this trail long enough to escape its gravitational pull depends on several factors: your genes and personality; the number of dopamine receptors in your brain; the drug's availability and your exposure to those who use it; the presence of a mental disorder; physical or sexual abuse suffered early in life. Addiction to opiates is rarely immediate; numerous tributaries offer themselves as exit routes but their number diminishes with each hit. Bizarrely, most people will experience heroin at some point in their lives, usually in the moments before death, when it's administered as morphine to ease the passage. Frequent users are forced to search for novel routes to the bloodstream as veins collapse. Alternating sites can prevent this, moving from inside the elbow, down the forearm – avoiding arteries, making sure vessels don't have a pulse – into the back of the hand or the palm if the pain can be tolerated, into the fingers. Stomach, groin, thigh, calf and feet are all feasible. Neck, breasts, face and genitalia all carry increased risk but offer a last resort when you've spent hours stabbing away at flesh. During his most prolific period as a junkie, he knew someone who once injected into her eye.

'Stay squeamish,' was her advice.

He places his tools in a plastic crate taken from the yard, leaving spares of those duplicated, enough for her to carry out rudimentary tasks. The landlord works on the principle of not bothering you if you didn't bother him, so tenants tended to make their own maintenance arrangements.

He will miss the flat, its allusion to a status of sorts. Thirty-five. Halfway along life's path and almost nothing to show. What had been his lot before it was reduced to suspended animation? Memories surface when he allows: helping his brother build the landscaping business; being rubbish in goal and laughing in the pub afterwards. Of everything it laid claim to, perhaps friendship was the keenest loss.

From the kitchen he hears the flat door open and close. He calls out her name, but by the time he emerges to explain the bin sacks, she has shut herself in the bedroom. Perhaps the shoplifting has resumed, the impulse to take what was not hers gaining new purchase. It occurs to him just to leave, the words he will utter gratuitous, the worst cliché. Why wound each other further? Better to retain a semblance of respect.

Her crying sounds theatrical, strident bursts that are more felt than heard. He finds her crouched beside the bed, the noise – not hers, he now sees – settling to a steady whimper, as if the heat forbade such effort. The baby's face radiates from a circled opening in the towel as Electra rocks it back and forth in an easy cadence. Small runnels form above its nose in a half-frown, its eyes blinking before fixing on nothing in particular. The thrum of music from below, coupled with the motion, appears to soothe the child, its bawling soon receding to nothing. Electra reconfigures the towel in order to place a finger in the baby's hand, which after a second or two it grips.

So this is a mirage, he thinks – the sun orchestrating

some divine revenge, a punishment befitting their crime. A glimpse at the unrealised. He says her name but she won't look at him.

'What have you done?'

She raises a hand to indicate the need for quiet, her febrile smile traversed by a single tear, her forearm blazed with the blistered track-marks that resemble one of the great constellations. He kneels down, careful not to get too close.

'Electra, where did you take it from?'

She cradles the bundle, humming softly now, his presence incidental. Leaning back he draws the curtain to keep the sun from them, the baby threatening to cry at the noise, before attending again to Electra's serenade. *If that mockingbird won't sing . . .*

He speaks more softly this time, placing a hand on her leg.

'We have to return it. I can take it back.'

She ignores him so he tries a different approach.

'It's too hot in here.'

He holds his arms out and she shifts back like some wild and frightened thing, tightening her grip. If there is any separating the two of them, it will not, he realises, happen without violence.

He supposes the child is a day or two old, its eyes in awe of each new sensation, the beginnings of a smile forming, its new world settled enough now to be of comfort. It won't always be this hot, he wants to announce, keen to apologise for the previous generation's decadence. Watching this absurd version of motherhood play out he allows a fantasy to form, one where such unfathomable gifts go unquestioned. Perhaps the world is reordered now; perhaps things like this happen.

He stands and Electra shoots him a look, eyes aflame in maternal defiance.

'It needs something to drink,' he says. 'Some milk or water.'

His apparent collusion relaxes her a little.

'What shall we call her?' Electra says.

In the kitchen he can hear more sirens and imagines the panic, the fretful scramble, wonders how someone can be so careless. This cigarette is harder to roll, his hands atremble, his body remembering a more potent remedy, one that begins in the poppy fields of Afghanistan and ends in such lavish misery. It was never really about the rush for him, the fabled fire that tore through his veins in euphoric rampage. More it was the sense of serenity, of being held, as if by a parent or lover, warm and cosseted, the day kept just enough at bay.

He looks out across the scorched city and thinks about the things people live for, the poison and love they depend on. He thinks about the young Romanian, how he'll keep his helmet on those extra few seconds now if he wants to see his child again. And he thinks about the call he will soon make, that will lure the sirens to them, that will make her hate him even more, perhaps forever. He will give her a few more minutes, though; he owes her that.

The Grandmaster of Gaza

He watches her contemplate the hole she's dug for herself, her impetuosity the prelude to another losing position. Morning sun dances on the ebony and boxwood pieces, a set carved in this room by her grandfather, his father, during the first intifada. It is flawless except for the black king's absent finial, lost to a falling section of wall when a tank shell struck the house across the street. He should repair it, find a wood that matches, though he is no artisan, lacking his father's elan for such matters. For now the piece's imperfection acts as a harbinger of white's early advantage, something his daughter is often profligate with.

Yasmeen retreats the bishop, huffs at the realisation her attack was ill-conceived.

'You have to anticipate all the outcomes,' he says. 'Don't be so easily lured by weakness.'

She pretends it is of little consequence, that another opening will present itself, optimism inherited from her mother. With practice she could be very good, perhaps as strong as her grandfather, who regularly beat the grand-masters of Europe and America in epic correspondence games. At the height of his prowess, there were invitations to tournaments and exhibitions around the world, but even when permission was granted for him to travel, he chose to stay, lauding his beloved city, the sea breeze that billowed in at night, the fresh tuna fishermen barbecued on the beach.

'Why would I leave?' he'd say.

They called his father the Grandmaster of Gaza, though he achieved no such rank officially, his status more one of quiet legend. It was said that by the age of six he could beat everyone at his school, and, a few years later, everyone this side of Tal al-Hawa. As worthy opponents became harder to find, he was enticed to the West Bank, to play in the cafés and marketplaces of Ramallah and Jenin, where wizened men four times his age and twice his size would marvel at the bravura of his gambits, the apparent recklessness of his sacrifices. He had no formal instruction, the game learned by watching others play at family gatherings, the house on Sundays a place of great theatre and revelry. When a game between uncles ended in a draw, he would often announce how one of them could have triumphed if only they'd persevered, demon-strating the sequence of moves to a mesmerised audience. Aged 12 he was invited to play a visiting Hungarian master, a series of games witnessed by half of Palestine, the legend went. Two defeats and a draw later, the man returned to Budapest broken and, it was said, never to play again.

His father's particular strength, his party piece, was playing multiple boards simultaneously, once going unbeaten against a circle of 16 players, drawing only four games. Or he would challenge the local champion blindfolded, the moves communicated to him verbally by an arbiter, his father playing to the crowd, pretending he'd lost track of the position before triumphing. His style, at a time when conservatism had come to dominate, was unswervingly aggressive, often sacrificing his queen in order to secure an outrageous win several moves later. He played quickly whether games were time controlled or not, and became renowned for his 'announced victories', remarking to an incredulous opponent, 'mate in five', artifice that solicited both admirers and enemies.

Yasmeen is bored now, the days without school long and empty. It is one thing to have an irritable teenager skulk about the house during evenings and weekends, quite another from dawn to dusk. He will send her to buy bird food later. They have been told the classrooms are too badly damaged to open for the new term, and so, in-between their games of chess, he gives her lessons at the kitchen table, indulging his daughter's appetite for knowledge. When the power is on – six hours a day, if they are lucky – he uses the computer given to them by a fan of his father's, watching British wildlife documentaries, a little of which he understands. Or he encourages her to write an essay on one of the novels she read last term, sometimes a story of her own. Science is her passion, but he knows little of how it's taught, and in moments of levity Yasmeen laughs at his clumsy attempts to do so. He hopes she will become a doctor, though talk of such is rare these days; it is hard to look too far ahead while death walks so brazenly among them. She will be offered counselling when the school finally reopens, as all children are, to deal with the trauma of the last fifty days, to come to terms with it. She will refuse.

He savours the last of his morning coffee. Warm air brings on it the sound of falafel crackling in the fryer run by the old man at the end of the street. It is a strange time, once the euphoria of a ceasefire recedes, the realisation it will take years, a decade perhaps, just to see the city returned to how it was in June. What has changed for the better, people ask, for surely this cannot have been for nothing. It will be different this time, goes the old lie. Rubbish collections stopped more than a month ago and have yet to resume, scores of feral cats and dogs amassing at the piles of detritus. Redolent of some medieval tableau, donkey carts have been deployed to collect what they can. Two weeks ago the pumping stations, bereft of fuel, stopped working and raw sewage now seeps into the streets, the sludge drawing throngs of flies. They say it will find a way into the water supply soon.

Gazans adapt, though; he sees it everywhere. One of

their neighbours runs a car on spent cooking oil, the waft of falafel and fries lingering in its wake. Others cram four at a time in the front seat of a taxi to get to work, the scene faintly comic. During the last war, when a shell killed the zoo's only zebra, the owner's son bought a white donkey, secured tape down its flanks and painted the gaps with black hair dye, the result a small zebra that brays. You make the best of things.

It was the Russians his father truly admired, though it was unclear whether he saw any of the greats play, his veneration of them likely coming from games he studied. Their influence even contributed to his most enduring affectation when playing, a subtle yet damning flourish that saw him grind a piece into the board after advancing it, unsettling the most stoic of opponents. As a child he would watch his father play out endless positions alone, studying alternative paths a game could have taken, scrutinising the pieces for hours as if they held the code to life. Notation to every game was documented with deliberate strokes of a fountain pen in his leather-bound journal, its pages handmade from the finest Italian paper, the cover held together by a burnished copper clasp. He would listen to coverage of high profile matches unfolding on the other side of the world, playing out the game himself as moves stole through on an old valve radio, the air rich with the odour of hot dust.

It was a surprise to everyone when his father stopped

playing, the set stowed away instead of adorning the alcove mid-game. Only when Yasmeen returned from school one day and requested he show her how to play, were the pieces retrieved.

He prepares their lunch, leaving Yasmeen eyeing his weakened king-side pawns. Food is more plentiful since the ceasefire – olives, dates and bread abundant again. He salivates at the thought of za'atar for breakfast in the coming days, of fresh sardines barely an hour from the ocean. There is a rumour it will be safe to fish again soon. Later he will head out to the lemon grove his own grandfather planted in the fifties, check this modest source of income has not been destroyed. It amazes him how fruitful these citrus trees are, how hardy they have become, despite the parched soil. Much of their best arable land falls inside the buffer zone, where they are forbidden to farm.

Work is harder to come by since the Egyptians flooded the tunnels at Rafah. He is not sorry, his body too beleaguered to be hauling livestock and fuel underground for half a mile in appalling conditions. It is a younger man's work. They say it is the biggest smuggling operation in the world, employing tens of thousands, a lifeline of their economy but also a death trap. Tunnel walls collapse, cables snap, fires break out. A cousin once tried to smuggle in a lion for the zoo. The animal, insufficiently sedated, awoke mid-tunnel, opening him up from neck to belly.

The day he started work there, the tunnel owner led him to a well shaft secreted inside a tent. Suspended above it was a crossbar with a pulley attached, below which hung a harness for lifting and lowering goods and people. As he sat in the harness, a spool of metal cable turned on a winch, lowering him the sixty feet into the twilit bowels of the earth. Five to ten of them worked twelve-hour shifts, day and night, six days a week, communicating with the owner via a two-way radio that had receivers throughout the tunnel. They earned around $50 a shift but could go weeks or months between payments.

And so an economy functions; not as others do, but money finds its way. He knew people who went by tunnel to the Egyptian side of Rafah for medical treatment, had heard of VIP routes for wealthy travellers, complete with air-conditioning and cell phone reception.

He misses the market at Rafah, the noise and fumes of generators blending with the braying of donkeys, the piquant smoke of shawarma spits, row upon row of stands selling all that had emerged from the tunnels.

Were Yasmeen interested in the history of her country, he'd tell her how it has always been fought over. By Pharaohs, Hebrews, Philistines, Persians, Alexander the Great, Romans, Byzantines, Arabs, Ottomans. Later still Napoleon, the British, the Egyptians. Armies marching into the desert relied on the city's fortress walls and gushing wells, while for merchants Gaza was a bountiful marine spur of the spice routes and agricultural trade.

Travellers sought out its inexpensive tobacco, its brothels; even now Israeli chefs covet Gaza's strawberries and quail. Invaders to the shores these days would be greeted by bullet-pocked buildings, skeletal seaside cafés and fetid tide pools, while inland abandoned Israeli settlements lie decaying, their fields sanded over, their greenhouses ramshackle, weatherworn. Gaza's airport, once a source of enormous pride, is now used only by herders grazing sheep, Bedouin feeding their camels.

He watches Yasmeen make a move and then retract it, a habit he needs to relieve her of. She loops a twine of hair round a finger in contemplation, every now and then emitting a sigh of self-admonishment at a strategy's shortcomings. Her face, he realises, has a new configuration these days, the puppy fat of childhood receding to leave an angular, more exacting beauty.

The shell that damaged the black king that day also took away her brother, Hasan, and their mother. They had been told it was safe to return, a window of calm in which to gather belongings, to leave the relative safety of the UN facility. Yasmeen was tired so stayed behind, her brother insisting he come to help.

Less than a second after the explosion, rubble from the neighbour's house surged through their windows and walls, half a home blasted into their own. When the air cleared and the ringing in his ears became something he could bear, he tried to stand but his legs would not obey him. Later, as he sat bleeding by the side of the road, he watched as someone carried his wife's body from the debris, laying her down beside him as if putting her to bed. The next day a crane removed large segments of the two homes that had become one. They found Hasan shortly before dusk.

One of the last shells to fall this time landed in the cemetery at Jabalia, the dead – though as far as he knows not his dead – forced to partake in the suffering of the living, their ashen bones scattered about broken grave-stones, in need of a second burying.

Yasmeen calls to him. She has made her move, a simple pawn push, subtle but one that strengthens her position mid-board. It is conservative and he smiles, placing their food on the table. Once again he vows to mend the black king, to locate the leather-bound journal documenting her grandfather's games. Chess, according to his father, is both art and science, the smoking out of an opponent's king rarely achieved with cunning and intuition alone, requiring flair and bravura also. He believed in its poetry, its grace. Its solemn beauty.

After lunch he will check on the birds. Last year, on what would have been his wife's forty-first birthday, he converted the space where Hasan's room once stood into an aviary, in which around twenty birds now dwell: pigeons, sparrows, hummingbirds, creatures injured in the fighting, brought to him in boxes or towels once word got out. He has become known as the Birdman, the one who fixes the birds, though most won't fly again. Some respond well, adapting to their internment; others fight it, fight each other. In time a few can be released, the ones he deems sufficiently recovered to survive, to take their chances. He asks those who bring them where the birds were found, in order to return them to the same patch of sky. He likes to watch them, their suspicion as he opens the door of the small wicker cage. There is a moment's hesitancy as the terrain is assessed, as they scan for predators, and then they are gone.

Scene Forty-Seven

She'd made it. He didn't recognise her name – she must have married – but there was something about her face, when she was doing disapproving or upset, that caught his attention. He'd assumed her career, like his, had stalled after the film. But there she was, some fancy US drama. What would she be now? Early forties. A little younger than himself, he remembered.

He got the email address through her agent. An old friend from England, he said, wanting to catch up.

'Hello,' he typed. 'I hope this finds you well.'

It had been his first role of any note, having previously scraped a living from fleeting but regular appearances in sitcoms, the occasional voiceover. She'd had a small part in that hospital drama, but was otherwise known for the stage.

The director, an unremarkable journeyman, was out to shock, to ruffle establishment feathers in the twilight of his career. He wanted relative unknowns to play the parts, so their egos didn't compromise his aesthetic vision for the piece. On three occasions during the audition he said *the scene* would be the main character.

'I'm not sure where to begin,' the email continued.

She clashed with the director for days beforehand, but he insisted the scene was integral, that it had to be done that way. The only concession she got was on the number of crew allowed on set that afternoon: two cameramen, someone on sound, and the director. She could pull out, she was told, but she'd likely not work again. He'd see to it.

'I saw you in that new series,' he typed. 'It's got a primetime slot over here. You've done really well.'

He'd played her lover, recently jettisoned. Scene forty-seven opened with an argument. 'Take me back,' he said over and over. 'I'll do anything.' 'I'm sorry,' she said, 'it's finished. There's someone else.'

The director kept talking about authenticity. He wanted the audience to experience what she felt. Shortly before filming, the director took him to one side. 'We can only do this once,' he said. 'I don't want you to hold back. Don't worry about what she says or does. We only stop when I say cut.'

The script was vague at this point: there were probably only half a dozen lines of direction between *Argument moves to bedroom* and CRAIG *leaves the flat*. 'Just go with it,' the director said. 'Draw on whatever you have to.'

It was the last scene they had together. He saw her on

set during the rest of the filming, but they hadn't spoken again.

'What's America like?' he wrote. 'You look . . .'

The reviews were polarised. One called it the most important artistic endeavour of the year. Another regarded it at gratuitous and sickening. Calls came for a ban, which were largely resisted. He never watched it.

The parts began to dry up. He acted for another year, maybe a little longer.

Pouring another drink, he deleted the email.

The Offspring Badge

The drive to his house takes me through a tunnel of arcing beeches, skeletal boughs writhing into one another above the car. The road itself falls away in a ribbon of mauve, earlier rain sheening its surface, the sluicing beneath me amplified by the trees. His directions had been comprehensive, overly helpful, and I imagine others receiving an abridged version, my navigational deficiencies still flung at me after all this time. Glancing at the printout of his words on the passenger seat, I note again the underlined advice: *If you reach the sculpture that looks like a scrotum, you've gone too far.* I'm tempted to drive on, to witness such a spectacle, but poor timekeeping was another stick he beat me with, albeit cloaked with banter, and so I take the sharp left as instructed, onto a single-track road. A mile or so later I see the lane as described, a thatched cottage a hundred yards along it, pretty without being quaint. Parking next to the only vehicle, an expensive-looking MPV complete with child seats in the rear, I fold up the directions, putting the sheet in the glove compartment as if it wasn't needed. I want to check my face and hair, but sense someone at the front door.

We meet mid-path, greet each other, then hug briefly, the gesture, although not entirely awkward, still a harbinger of the nine years that have passed. It wasn't mentioned on the phone but I assume we're alone, his wife at work or courteously absent, the children he spoke of at pre-school. Perhaps he assumed correctly that I knew of their existence – a boy and girl, a year apart – but the nonchalance with which he announced them was at best insensitive.

'Come in,' Ben says. 'Just making coffee.'

The kitchen smells of freshly-baked bread and jam, a large rustic table still adorned with the delights of a lavish breakfast. A noticeboard is dominated by a child's painting, a crude watercolour of some nondescript creature, limbs and teeth in abundance.

'This is lovely,' I say, looking around.

'It wasn't when we moved in. Jaz is the creative one. Saw through the rising damp and rubble. She did most of it herself.'

Hearing her name abbreviated is somehow another small cut in a year of unrelenting assaults. I'd found some small humour in the unabridged version when a mutual friend uttered it, knowing how Ben would once have found it pretentious. Jasmine. Delicate and fragrant. But who apparently turns her hand to property development in between motherhood and a dynamic career.

'Do you still take sugar?'

I nod, assuming this to be sufficient, though apparently it isn't.

'Two, please.'

He pours the beans into an antique grinder and I have to stifle a laugh as he struggles with the mechanism, beans spilling out onto the flagstones, hopping around us in a chaotic beat.

'Jaz's preserve, I'm afraid. There's a technique.'

'Instant is fine,' I say.

The log burner draws my eye, not because it's the room's focal point, but lying before its bronzed flicker, asleep on the rug, is a dog: a mature Border collie crossed with something, perhaps a spaniel. The last time I saw Ben, he'd driven up to the cottage I shared with my then husband, his visit to observe the last rites for a dog we'd got together, that I'd taken with me when I left him. For a moment, this revelation hurts more than the evidence of a family – because the breed is similar, because the roles are so manifestly reversed now, I'm unsure.

'Lazy thing,' Ben says. 'Only goes out when it has to. Lets the kids climb all over him, though.'

The animal lifts its head, acknowledges my presence, then returns to the business of slumber. I want to stroke it, feel the warmth deep in its coat, but Ben's casual allusion to the dog suggests it's more Jasmine's or the children's than his, and so I head to the window, gaze out at the garden.

'That's next year's project.'

'It's lovely,' I say, revolted by my sycophancy, my inability to find another adjective.

'The children want a pond, but there's not been time. Do you know anything about ponds?'

I shake my head, force a smile. The coffee is good, too good for instant, and I sense the best of everything is indulged here, a decadence he'd have ridiculed back then. I'd like a real drink, something he would once have offered a guest, despite it only being midday. *Carpe* the *vinum*, as he liked to say.

Ben's face has weathered, the final vestige of youth flown at forty, although there's a case for his being more handsome now, threads of grey behind his temples adding a note of distinction. Contentment seems to hold him.

'I was sorry to hear about you and Peter,' he says.

It feels too soon in my visit for condolence, though Ben's words sound genuine. He'd every right to a lingering smugness, my infidelity – the overlap, if you will – never fully articulated, but felt by him, I'm sure. I see now, more than ever, how that day he came to see the dog must have been insufferable, my life with Peter on display in all its attendant happiness, the dying animal an unsubtle emblem of it all.

'I'm fine,' I say, the lie tiresome these days and presumably transparent. If Ben is at all smug, he hides it well.

Nobody ever tells you how numbing divorce is, how inert it leaves you, the silence once cherished in parts of the house now condemning as you struggle to conceive how life will be lived. They don't tell you how much you'll miss marriage's easy boredom.

At first, after the verdict was delivered, Peter played well the part of considerate husband.

'It doesn't matter,' he said. 'We've got each other, that's the important thing.'

He told me what I needed to hear, clichés delivered with precise timing, and for weeks I think I believed him. Perhaps he believed them himself, for who can account for the implications of such news immediately? Or maybe he simply denied the results, the reality some temporary affliction visited upon us, a problem science and medicine would soon solve. Either way, the permanence of my condition began to fester in him, decades without a family of his own stretching out, barren and without purpose, without legacy. I think I not only became redundant in his eyes, but a source of misery, our future burdened with the cargo of my infertility. The final time we made love, his movements verged on violence, as if this could compensate for my shortcoming. A battering ram to breach the sterile defences.

The garden isn't as neglected as Ben makes out and for a moment I imagine what I'd plant, this being *my* preserve, at least it was before Peter's solicitor instructed the sale of our cottage. The letter stated I could buy him out, if I was so inclined, to which I replied inclination had little to do with it. But even if an unlikely windfall bequeathed itself, how could I have stayed, cohabiting with ghosts? By comparison my parents' garden, modest and manicured, requires little more than the neighbour's weekly attention with the mower in summer. I've offered to perform this duty for as long I'm there, but it would risk offence apparently. My mother is kind enough not to mention the future, ask how long I'll be staying. And she hides well her disappointment at the theft of grand-parenthood. Is that a word?

I can hardly remember Ben's lovemaking style. Certainly never violent. A little too tender, I think. Too considerate.

I'm ambivalent about the prospect of seeing a photo-graph of Jasmine, curious yet uneasy. Attractive in a classical way, a thoughtless friend described her. Younger as well. A Nobel Prize winner in waiting, no doubt. How will Ben describe me to her later? I'm no threat, of course, but he'll still have to play it carefully, choose the right words, somewhere between indifference and disdain. *Oh, you know, she looked older. Bigger.*

Ben shuffles about the room, perhaps wondering how long I'll stay, my standing unnerving him.

'How's the business going?' I ask. 'Have you still got the canoes?'

'We sold up, got an offer that was hard to turn down. I went back to teaching.'

I try to hide my surprise, my disappointment at his returning to a world he despised.

'Don't you miss the great outdoors? Being your own boss?'

'It was hard work, insecure. I'm at a good school now.'

Our conversing allows me to scan the room a little and I see a photograph on the bookcase, a family portrait in monochrome, trendily artistic. Even in this glance I get a sense of Jasmine's beauty, which now fills the lounge like a gas. I wonder who Peter has upgraded to, knowing he couldn't be single for five minutes, how the prospect terrified him. Perhaps he conducted interviews, a one-question assessment to filter out the unfruitful. He would have us come with a badge, a sign alluding to our status, a use-by date, so there's no ambiguity. *This is what you'll be letting yourself in for. These are the miles on the clock.* Perhaps a contract would work, clear and binding, either party able to withdraw if terms weren't met. *Caveat emptor.*

There are days I think I'm the only single person, the wildcard when all the pairs have been gathered up – cat ownership, bingo and a wardrobe of frumpy clothes imminent. Yet the thought of dating appals me, its insufferably polite and contrived dance: *What do you do for a living? How about hobbies? Do you want children one day?* Yes, I'm thinking of stealing one. How about you?

I put Ben out of his misery and sit on the sofa, whereupon he takes the armchair. The dog stretches, rolls a quarter turn away from the heat, belly up, its downy penis lolling askance.

'Antique?' I say, smoothing a hand along the sofa's lustrous leather.

'Not sure. Jaz would know.'

Of course she would.

When I was pregnant, in that other life, it had all felt too easy, as if none of it had been earned. We got a small but charming flat by the river; Ben finished his training, took a job nearby. At weekends I painted and we walked the dog. It wasn't planned, but I still thought he would welcome the news, greet with wonder this shift to some exciting new realm. Our straight line would become a triangle, something with form and shape. With volume. A third-person narrative, if you like.

I wonder what labels I will now endure, what assumptions people will make of my childless state. I'll have to pursue some high-flying vocation in order to justify my existence. *She didn't have time for children. Not the type.* Will I convene with other such women, converse about how we don't need to give birth for our lives to have meaning, that some women choose to, others not? How it's not the be all and end all. Other things will enrich us. What a funny phrase, be all and end all.

I swill the last of my coffee around, try to remember what closure I thought could be found here today.

'Are you seeing anyone new, then?' Ben asks.

The enquiry seems sincere, in that it possesses no

agenda, though what is it they say, about wanting former lovers to be happy but not that happy?

'No, not really,' the 'not really' so as not to appear entirely tragic.

'Loving the single life, hey?'

Something like that.

I realise there are no books, at least in the rooms I've seen, and I wonder if this is another concession to Ben's new life, Jasmine conducting a cull when they moved in together, perhaps keeping a Tolstoy or two for display. It was the one thing we divided up easily, literature rarely bought or received as a couple. Ben seemed always to accept I was taking the dog, his powers of reason diminished by then.

I want to use the bathroom but I suppose it will be full of further homely trappings: toothbrushes, bath toys, perfumes. Doors to bedrooms might lie ajar, the opportunity for further flagellation irresistible as I'm lured moth-to-flame, bringing a tiny jumper to my nose, inhaling that most unique of scents. Perhaps I would take something, a memento giving some small illusion of recompense. I wonder what sort of father Ben is, if such things can be graded. Is he like TV dads – nurturer, care-giver, sharing evenly hunter-gatherer duties? At bedtime reading does he affect with precision characters' voices, conceding easily to requests for one more story? Do they go to him to clean and bandage scrapes in the knowledge he's gentler, more patient?

Ben's voice brings me back.

'Have you far to go this afternoon?'

For a second I forget the fabrication I'd woven, a nearby meeting management insisted I attend, how I recalled Ben lived in the area, that we should catch up if he was free.

'A few miles, back towards the coast.'

'You want some lunch? There's soup left from the weekend.'

I said I thought we'd be given something there. Again I wish he'd offer me a drink, pour us both something befitting this unlikely congregation I've fashioned from an incautious email.

I wonder if I occupy any of his thoughts these days, whether he remembers heading up to London at dawn that time, weeks before I became pregnant, marching with a thousand others, feeling part of something bigger than ourselves, the sense of comradeship, of trying to change the world, not for us, but for those to come. How we ran from police and hid in that Lebanese taverna, getting drunk, laughing with waiters, leaving once the streets had quietened, walking for hours until dawn bled over the city.

I suspect, though, that he doesn't indulge nostalgia, his life replete with the forging of new marvels. *Damnatio memoriae.*

The day of the abortion, Ben took the morning off work. I'd said he didn't need to, playing down the emotion I felt, agreeing that it was the pragmatic thing to do, a mutual decision, which it had seemed at the time. Only later was I aware of the manipulation, his chipping away, his reasoning – he could reason anything given a half-sympathetic ear: *It's too early in our relationship, the timing isn't right, better when things are more stable, once we've travelled.* I hadn't realised we were unstable. Or is it instable? I never know. I almost changed my mind on that last morning, perhaps some instinctive awakening, a chemical entreaty, unknown to science, deep inside me. I'd even begun talking to it, trying out names to see how they fitted. It was the size of a walnut, I read later. Not yet a person, though, Ben kept saying.

Years later, when Peter and I sat in front of the specialist, I knew what was coming, whose fault it would be. Who was faulty. He squeezed my hand when the verdict was delivered, but I could sense relief in his grip, that despite the condemnation of us as a couple, he had been given a reprieve, his seed beyond reproach.

So what will my gift to the world be now? Even if some latent artistic talent makes itself known, there's hardly time to carve out an *oeuvre*. What a wonderful image!

I used to think love was an achievement in itself, its status acquired from the sum of one's virtues, a badge sewn to your sleeve beneath 'career' and above 'offspring'. Perhaps I'll discover I can sing and appear on one of those awful talent shows, the token late bloomer. I could get a tattoo or move abroad and follow some fashionable religion. If my brother ever matures enough to breed, I could make aunt-hood my *raison d'etre*, savour the joyous moments, unencumbered by any lingering duty.

Ben smiles through the silence that's gathered, perhaps regretting my presence now that curiosity has receded.

'Another coffee?'

Perhaps I should tell him my fate. That the choice he was so keen I made back then was a luxury I won't have again. I wonder what names his are bestowed with, whether he stole from the mock list we made when there was no consequence. Maybe Jasmine was keen to retain a floral theme. It must be difficult, to achieve something distinctive yet not outlandish. Perhaps I even snuck in there as a middle name, a surreptitious concession to first love, one he'd share with his daughter when she was old enough to value such sly disloyalty, to regard it eccentric. Such a fuss made over first love, when it's last love that matters – assuming the two aren't the same, which they rarely are.

I'm glad the photograph suggests both are able-bodied, my wish for otherwise made shortly after Peter had left and on hearing about Ben's incipient fatherhood. Anguish makes such spiteful fools of us.

'I should probably be going,' I say. 'My meeting.'

Ben rises a little too quickly. The dog opens its eyes but remains impassive. I realise that I really miss his parents; one can quibble over the division of CDs and friends, but parents are rather assigned, aren't they?

We walk to my car in the clean early-afternoon light, the sky now blue as blue gets. A gustless breeze stirs the last of the tree's leaves until they let go. At its base a blackbird prospects in the grass.

A last look at it all. Despite appearances I suppose there are cracks even here.

We hug until I release him.

'Good luck with that pond,' I say.

Banging Che Guevara

CLIVE – TANYA – ROZ

Once a week Clive takes the new intern to a hotel in Covent Garden. Furthering the frisson is the knowledge his wife would be appalled at the price of rooms there.

As her head nods repeatedly up and down like a donkey's, Tanya wonders if all men his age have such obvious odour issues. His age being roughly that of her father's.

The note says he'll be late home again. This would have bothered Roz once; now it comes as a source of pleasure. She will light some candles, have a long bath and open one of his expensive reds.

Perhaps he should join a gym, get in shape. Last night he read about hair transplants, how a strip of the scalp is harvested from the back of the head, divided into individual follicles, then inserted into small holes in the crown. Like a vegetable garden.

You have to make sacrifices, Tanya tells herself, if you want to get to the top. It's just a bit of fun. Right on cue, he turns her over.

On Saturdays, when Clive is 'at the office', she spends the afternoons watching her father dribble as he plays gin rummy with others in the care home. She'd like to speak of her decision but the words would likely kill him.

He is fascinated by the new tattoo of Che Guevara on her lower back, the way the face contorts and smiles a little as he pounds away. Roz hates them, of course. Perhaps he should get one, something tribal, or his name in Sanskrit. He will ask Tanya's advice after.

Tanya knows how the industry works. It's not *what* you know. Shutting her eyes, trying not to breathe through her nose, she pretends it's the guy from marketing, the one with the shoulders.

She married too young. Or too something. It was what you did, especially when 'impure' thoughts threatened to take root, thoughts that scared you but which were now more established than the large sycamore across the road. And it is time to blossom.

*

Clive can't help himself; it's in his nature. And you shouldn't deny your nature. He has needs. It's not as if his wife is interested in such matters any more. It's probably grown over.

Once promoted, Tanya will break it off gently. And then focus on Shoulders. Within a year they will marry and have beautiful children. She feels sorry for people without goals.

Roz has a secret that no one knows. Not her late mother, her incontinent father. Nor her children. She should probably ask Clive to sit down before telling him tonight. She would like a picture of his expression.

Che's grin is mocking him now. And with every third or so slap against Tanya's arse, he appears to wink, to egg him on. It's as if he's banging Che Guevara.

Her boss has normally come by now. That was what made it bearable, the brevity. She issues words of encouragement, tells him he's a tiger, says she's hot for him, that it's the best she's had. If they're done by half past, she can buy that new top in River Island before it closes.

She first saw her at yoga class a month ago, wild-haired and serene, a goddess. It was like being a teenager again. She came home and practised Inverted Tortoise until the thoughts left. At class the following week, the woman caught her staring and smiled.

Clive will google it later. It had never been a problem before. He'll order something to be delivered at work, something to prolong his rigid state. Che, meanwhile, looks appalled.

If Shoulders puts up resistance, she will bring out the killer heels. They had only failed on one previous occasion, and that was hardly her fault. And there was always Shoulders's colleague in Accounts to fall back on.

Last week she decided she would leave him the cat. That was last week. He can keep the car, the house, the silly device that dries salad leaves, but not the cat.

He tells Che: 'She just doesn't appreciate how hard I work. Her only stress comes from choosing what to cook.' He wonders what's for dinner.

Perhaps faking her own will help.

She hopes the cat will be OK in the new flat. Butter on its paws, a friend told her, when she first lets it out. Will margarine work?

Despite everything – her milky skin, her perfect breasts –

Che has toppled his erection. Overthrown it. What he needs, what he really needs, is the whole Bolivian army to silence his smug face. Or something to put over him.

Faking failed.

The children will have to divide their time when they come home now. She suspects, eventually, they'll find it amusing. Progressive.

In the lobby, as Clive checks out, the woman at the desk gives him that knowing look. He would like to tell her what he cleared last year after tax. He looks round for Tanya, to ask about tattoos, about the file he needs ready by Monday, but can't see her.

River Island is closed. She looks longingly at the shoes in the window, imagines she has just spent the afternoon with Shoulders.

Her last night in the family home. The neighbours will dine on the scandal for months, rally round Clive 'at this difficult time'. After finishing packing, she pours more wine and slips into the bath, wondering what it will feel like, with a woman.

Romi & Romina:
An Enquiry into Morals

She termed it ironic, though I suspect that wasn't correct. How the one thing the human mind could not comprehend was itself. She didn't mean the brain – that clod of moist beige tissue had apparently given up most of its secrets in the last few decades – but consciousness itself, which quite reasonably, she said, could be nothing more than a conjuring trick. And given our ignorance as to its origin, whether it even possessed a physical entity or not, it was entirely possible everything was sentient: cats, birds, insects. And without evidence consciousness required a brain at all, there was no logical reason to draw the line there. Plants, cars and desks could all be aware of their plantness, carness and deskness, merely unable to communicate it.

'Evolution,' she said, 'could easily have produced creatures atom-for-atom the same as humans, capable of everything we are, just with no flicker of self-awareness.' Such were the overtures Romina brought home from work and offered up as I attended to some unremarkable aspect of domestic life.

We'd met in a floating jazz bar down on the river, one of those trendy, ubiquitous places inhabited by the city's great and good, at least until another venue became de rigueur. I was neither adverse to the prospect of a relationship – short-term or otherwise – nor seeking one, and although Romina wasn't particularly my type, the encounter soon gained volition of its own, fuelled for the most part by her bizarre opening gambit. Once she'd established a physical attraction to someone, Romina's method was simple: she produced from her jeans pocket a Trivial Pursuit card and proceeded to reel off questions, seemingly oblivious to the unorthodoxy of such courtship. Men (and, I would later learn, the occasional woman) who correctly answered three or four out of six were worthy of further enquiry; ones and twos, she would tell me, were deemed stupid, fives and sixes too clever for their own good. Owing to the sizeable gaps in my general knowledge, our interaction almost ended there, my own score of three achieved thanks only to a guess at the number of moons to orbit Venus. Answer: none. My prize was an endless succession of tequilas and a tour of Romina's favoured nocturnal haunts, where we danced deep into the night like chemically-charged teenagers. After parting around 3am, I walked home beneath a pre-dawn sky suspecting life had been reordered for ever.

Within a week Romina introduced me to the intricacies of shadow puppet sex. From the precise configuration of our hands and fingers, we made the backlit semblance of two beings, furnishing one – usually but not exclusively mine – with male genitalia, before having them converge mid bedroom wall, my little finger thrusting back and forth to our feigned bursts of pleasure.

'You've got no stamina,' she said as the smallest digit of my left hand cramped prematurely. 'My shadow wants an orgasm.'

A fortnight later Romina evicted her flatmate of several years to accommodate my burgeoning collection of vinyl, the bookcase my father had built in the workshop of a psychiatric ward, and my perpetually indifferent Maine Coon, which would run away the following Bonfire Night. (A year later I would see the cat in a terraced window a mile from our home, looking as content and stupid as ever.) Moving into Romina's on a rainy Tuesday in March, I passed her flatmate as she heaved a series of swollen bin sacks into the side of a waiting van. I offered to help but the woman stopped only to spit in my face before continuing.

'You met Lucia, then?' Romina said as I began unpacking.

It was the first time I'd lived with anyone beyond my parents or a pair of Portuguese art students who liked to create collages from each other's pubic hair, an example of which now hung in a gallery across town. The shadow sex continued for a while, but never matched for romance or audacity that first occasion. By way of reparation the non-shadow version proved more gratifying than any I'd known, Romina's libido equal to that of her puppet's. With precise and presumably proficient instruction, I was introduced to all manner of novel positions, our body parts acquainted with one another in increasingly fanciful ways. It was several days before we came up for air, acknowledging that it might prove beneficial to learn something about each other beyond our basic geometry and a shared loathing of Tom Hanks films. Romina, it turned out, was a post-doctoral philosophy researcher looking at the origins of moral behaviour. In particular she had just been funded to lead a multi-disciplinary project that ran a virtual human from birth to death, modelling every conceivable social, biological and emotional stimuli someone might experience, while observing the ethical judgements it made throughout life and the behaviours this led to. She listened with unconvincing interest to my endeavours as a reporter for the local paper, a job I managed to make sound even more prosaic than usual. From habit, or to deflect my intellectual inadequacies, I found succour in the journalist's lexicon.

'How does it work?'

'We program it to take in stimuli – sound, speech, visuals – to process them into data structures, which can then interact with each other to create unique associations.'

'Sounds complex.'

'Not really. All we do is define how the external input is stored and processed. Output is then monitored by several layers of the CPU neural processor to simulate the conscious and subconscious mind. It's just a series of gateways. In theory we can find out what informs people's moral choices.'

'You mean whether being an evil shit is innate or not?'

'More than that. The capacity for moral reasoning is evolutionarily ancient, but moral codes are culturally-specific. For example, once we're more familiar with the program, we could run Hitler's life. Or Stalin's. We could intervene at key moments, alter some facet or other, see what impact it has. Conversely, we could model someone deemed to have led a virtuous life and modify their childhood, weave in some disturbance or psychopathy.'

'Create a monster?'

'A virtual one, yes.'

'But a machine can't demonstrate moral autonomy; even I know they're just slaves to their programs.' I didn't especially know this, but it sounded good.

'Ethical behaviour is really just rule following, using our own programs. The idea that right and wrong, good and evil exist in some abstract sense, independent from humans who come to perceive them, is frankly bollocks.'

'So you input a load of experience and then ask it stuff?'

'Sort of. Computational morality has come a long way since the early days of AI. It's still a little like encoding a chess computer, yes, only now we can enter emotions and personality and regret into the algorithms. The system has a chip that works the same way our neural networks do. So far we've engineered three million fake neurons, connecting them with a billion fake synapses.'

'Is that a lot? It sounds a lot.'

'Still less intelligent than your cat, but it's a start. There's even a cynicism function we're developing.'

'What, you upload famous political speeches?'

'Not a million miles away. The breakthrough was creating a computer capable of bad things, yet able to choose not to do them. Or vice versa. We bring her to life next week.'

'Does she have a name?'

'Romina, of course.'

'Isn't that confusing?'

'She's Romi for short.'

I assumed Romi would be merely an array of computers and servers, or something running on a complex intranet, but she turned out to have a very physical presence on the one occasion I met Romina for lunch in her lab. The team had fashioned a particularly convincing android and from a distance it was indistinguishable from the woman I now shared my life with. Her lavish russet hair was tied back in the same chaotic manner, complete with a brace of rebellious tousles that framed her face, her posture as she sat cross-legged in an old Chesterfield one of quiet dignity.

Romi's life-sized body, Romina told me, was only capable of a few rudimentary movements; it was her dark interior that held untold wonderment. A ponytailed man named Ray explained with a partial stammer how Romi's face was the masterpiece, how technology that barely existed five years ago now allowed for something so human in appearance. Bestowed with a special silicon skin, the features were controlled by animatronic muscles that worked to move Romi's eyes and drive her expressions. She could make eye contact and convey a range of emotions, including empathy, sadness and irritation. Ray described how her skin even responded to touch and that she could experience pain, or at least a programmed response to it.

'What do you think of her?' asked Romina.

'The likeness is uncanny,' I said, which seemed to please everyone. 'She's beautiful.'

'Correct answer, although I could never really pull off that dress.'

'I thought the experiment was more . . . psychological. More virtual.'

'She was built by a Japanese robotics professor; his team flew over to take a plaster cast of my face. It meant more funding this way: we raise their profile, they raise ours. Of course this is just her façade.' Romina nodded to an elaborate system of PCs that connected wirelessly to the android. 'All the functions to do with movement and response are inside her, but what you think of as consciousness lies in the server farm over there. Eventually, when quantum processors become practical, it can all move inside her.'

'Impressive.' The team seemed to take this to mean the project per se, but it was Romi herself, her sheer presence, that I found so mesmerising, so unnerving.

'Computers these days regularly pass the Turing Test,' Romina continued. 'Their abilities double every six months. In ten years they'll be more intelligent than us on any given measure. In a hundred years they'll have more brain-power than all the humans ever to have walked the planet combined. They already make superior juries than us.'

'How so?'

'Using Bayesian logic a computer is more reliable than humans in the verdicts it reaches. The point is they don't have to always be right, just better than us.'

I looked at Romi, sitting impassively. 'She's less talk-ative than you.'

'Ask her something,' Romina said.

'Like what?'

'Anything. Introduce yourself first.'

I felt silly, especially with the others looking on, and wondered if some elaborate prank was playing out.

'Hello Romi, I'm Daniel.'

Romi's face turned smoothly, silently through ninety degrees, the eyes adjusting to meet mine.

'Can she see me?' I asked.

'Not in the sense you mean,' said Ray. 'But yes.'

When it spoke, the voice was more synthetic than I'd

expected, which was somehow comforting. 'Hello Daniel. My name is Romina, but you can call me Romi.'

'We can make her voice more realistic,' the real Romina said, 'more like mine, but it was a little weird.'

I asked Romi what the meaning of life was.

'I'm sorry Daniel, I don't understand. Perhaps you would like to ask me something else.'

Romina flashed me a scowl. 'Try again.'

'Hello, Romi,' I said. 'How many moons does Venus have?'

'Venus is the second planet from our sun and is named after the Roman goddess of love and beauty. It has no natural satellites.'

'You've tried her on the Trivial Pursuit card, then?'

'Not much point: she has access to every online encyclopaedia and search engine. I'm thinking of sending her to conferences in my place.'

'She'd have to do sarcasm.'

'We're working on it.'

Seeing Romina – the real one – that day, standing beside her unearthly doppelgänger, immersed utterly in the glorious complexities of her subject, led to a couple of realisations: first, that I had fallen unswervingly in love with her; and second, that this would only ever be reciprocated in part, the bulk of life's voltage for her found in the pursuit of knowledge and a quest to understand it. Love, for Romina, belonged to a more trivial stratum of experience, the deeper layers of meaning and value beyond its reach. It wasn't entirely fair to term her a stubborn rationalist: more that love's riddle, as with the existence of God, would never reveal itself, no matter the level of scrutiny. You simply believed in it or you didn't. We argued frequently about this – love not God; I shared her incredulity for the latter – battles that came with accusations of my quixotic nature, as she termed it.

'Don't take it personally,' she once said. 'I'm very fond of you.'

'I want to try something with our firstborn,' was how a pregnant Romina announced it one weekend in bed with the Sunday papers. From what I gathered, the project with Romi had run into trouble thanks largely to a paper by a Swedish neuroethicist who had ridiculed the team's methods. Even Romina conceded that results had at best been ambiguous, and it was rumoured the Japanese now wanted to disassociate themselves from the morality element. Starting a family had not been planned, but I hoped it would prove a welcome distraction for her.

'Something?'

'An enquiry.'

'You mean an experiment?'

She went on to describe the history of feral children, infants who'd been found in the woods, naked and scavenging, apparently without family, their pasts unfathomable. Such children were typically mute and did not understand the language of their rescuers (or captors, depending on your view). Some even walked quadrupedally. Efforts to integrate them proved mixed, with a few rehabilitating fully; others, though, led reclusive lives, the consequences of emotional and linguistic deprivation irreversible. The problem with both groups was that neither could shine any light on the origins of their wildness. And without the ability to monitor their previous existence, nor could they assist much with the enquiries scientists and philosophers aspired to make. At least not beyond that which could be gleaned from children with learning difficulties. Further, those who did respond to cognitive instruction had become tainted as witnesses, the socialisation destroying all essence of wildness. Either way scientists would often abandon the project, leading to claims that the child, instead of spending a considerable time living outside of organised human society, was merely the victim of neglect or some other emotional trauma. Nonetheless, according to Romina, fascination with such cases persisted through the ages, offering, in theory, a unique potential to study what made someone human.

'I want to take it a step further,' she said. 'I want to find out if moral instinct can develop without instruction.'

'I think there are laws preventing that.'

'It will only be for a few years.'

'You want our child to grow up in the woods?'

'Now you're being silly. Think of the possibilities. We

could create a new language, one that was morally bereft. No guidance of any kind about what was right or wrong.'

'I never know when to take you seriously.'

We didn't get the chance to run any philosophical experiments on our child – a seven and a half pound girl called Celeste – as Romina was killed three months after the birth. The van driver told police he had no chance, that she'd pulled out without looking, a witness claiming she'd been using her phone. The young policewoman who came to the house spoke in a soft and faltering voice. I'd thought it apocryphal, how your legs buckle from under you in such moments, but it isn't. Later I learned that the impact was so overwhelming, our car was compressed to a third of its size. Even now I think about those two-thirds.

Grief took several forms in the coming months. A doctor told me it had to run its course, like a virus; friends were equally unoriginal in their counsel. Decisions lined up like attack dogs: how long should I keep her possessions? What did I tell Celeste when she was old enough to understand? Each time I found some small strength, some cruel intervention conspired to break it: I'd find a swathe of Romina's hair while unblocking the hoover, or a voice on the phone would ask if she wanted to renew her gym membership. Such callers were subjected to a tyranny I hardly knew existed in me.

Photographs were both a source of comfort and torment, the temptation to delete them tussling with a desire to have more. The world itself seemed realigned, no longer adhering to the same scientific principles. Time refused my attempts to function within it; even inertia felt beyond me as the anguish claimed a little more each day. I needed Romina's direction, her tutelage, to function in life; she'd been the guiding lines that bled through my writing paper. One evening I observed Celeste watching me weep, envying her brain's inability to comprehend what had been lost.

It was a year or so after the funeral when Ray called. His stammer more pronounced, he told me the project had been put on hold – the funding withdrawn due to a lack of what he called 'empirical progress' – but that they hoped to relaunch it in the future. Obviously with a different android, he was quick to say. We chatted for a while, the emotion kept in check by small talk, evasive subjects such as my paper's feature on cuts to the University, how poorly the local football team was doing. I told him I hadn't been back to work, that fatherhood was sufficient for now. After a bloated silence he asked if I wanted to have Romi, to take her home once they'd disconnected her. I sensed his discomfort at asking what was surely a unique question.

'Don't the Japanese want her back?'

'Technology's moved on so much, she's a little redundant now.'

The thought had crossed my mind, though I imagined

she would come without any software, what essence of humanity she possessed diminished. She would be little more than a mannequin, a stuffed pet housed in the corner of a room, a macabre memento mori. The idea was both thrilling and revolting.

I thanked Ray for the offer. 'I'd like to see her again, though,' I said. 'We'd like to see her.'

It felt a huge risk taking Celeste to see Romi. Ray met us on campus and we headed to a smaller building on the University's fringes.

'Priorities have shifted,' he said. 'There's just me now really. A few students use her for their theses.'

I lifted Celeste from her buggy, which we left in the foyer, and carried her down some stairs into the basement, Ray leading the way through artificially-lit, airless corridors.

'What money there is,' he said, 'goes to cellular medicine these days.'

As we headed deeper into the building, I sensed a tension in Celeste – at this unfamiliar man, at a place she didn't know – and I tried to exude a nonchalance, despite the sweat rising on my back, my lungs vacuum-packed. The room itself was sparsely filled, a few work stations dotted around, one of the strip lights above them flickering on and off. In the far corner I saw Romi in her armchair, Romina's dress that she wore last time replaced with tracksuit bottoms and a jumper I didn't recognise, a modification perhaps made by the team after the accident, or by Ray this week to spare me.

'She's still connected to the server farm,' Ray said, 'but we share it with several other departments now.'

'So who is she this month: Myra Hindley or Mother Teresa?'

'We haven't run a character for months. She's just Romi for now.'

We stood there for a moment, the three of us. The four of us. In the silence Ray shifted his weight from leg to leg, and for the first time I got how difficult this was for him.

'Shall I boot her up?' he said.

He headed over to one of the desks, inserted an index finger into the computer's security reader before focusing on the screen. A minute or so later the soft buzz of motors and servos started up within Romi – life bestowed in a few clicks. Despite the absence of eyelids – or whatever gives the eye its embodiment – there was still a palpable shift in Romi's gaze from her unawakened state. Ray negotiated the mouse some more and she turned her head, the camera behind her eye scanning for potential inter-action, her stare finally settling on us. A moment later she smiled.

'Hello Daniel,' she said.

'She remembers me?'

'Of course,' said Ray. 'Visual recognition is old hat.'

I turned my daughter around, extended my arms a little. 'Romi, this is Celeste.'

'Hello Celeste. I'm Romi.' Romi's voice had changed since I was last here, was now entirely human, although there was nothing of Romina within it. Despite this Celeste seemed intrigued, her unease falling away as she fixed on this new but not new person in front of her. I wondered if she recognised Romi, remembered on some primitive level the alignment and proportions of her mother's face a year on. What *was* retained from those first few months mother and daughter shared? I presumed, that without the aid of photographs, nothing. A thought: perhaps we should keep her after all, take her home. We could set a place for her at the table, bring her out for birthdays, Sunday drives, parents' evenings. Ray could advise how to restore Romina's voice, Celeste utilising Romi's infinite knowledge for her homework. A mother of sorts. And, when the nights became incessant and devastating, as they still could on occasion, I could curl into her and forget. Show her how to make shadow puppets on the wall.

I encouraged Celeste to say hello but she didn't, whether sensing the absurdity of it or from shyness, it was hard to say.

'Would you like to ask me something?' said Romi.

Several things came to mind: why weren't you looking that day in the car? How can I do this on my own? What if I meet someone else? *We* meet someone else? Instead I looked hard at her face, on some level grateful to have this moment science had granted us. Had I been alone in the room, I almost certainly would have touched her, kissed her. Plunged my face deep in her hair in search of a fragrance I would never smell again.

Watching this bizarre scene play out, I realised something was missing. 'Can she laugh?' I asked Ray. He thought about this for a moment, before shaking his head, a trace of disappointment crossing his face at realising the oversight. I conducted a mental trawl of footage on my phone – not as much as I'd like, but something – and realised I had no record of her laughter.

'I'm sorry,' Ray said.

I smiled, then asked, 'What will happen to her?'

'Someone will dismantle her, recycle the parts.'

I pictured this image, tried hard to read something profound in it.

As we said goodbye I pulled Celeste closer, thought how much more I'd have fallen apart in her absence.

'Goodbye,' Romi said. 'I look forward to talking some more with you soon.'

I promised Ray I'd keep in touch, saw he knew that I wouldn't.

As we emerged into the winter sun and a tide of buoyant students, it seemed important to remember every word Romina had ever said, to document as much of her as I could, capture and keep it alive for our daughter.

'Soon there won't be anything only humans can do,' Romina once told me. 'By the end of the decade, computers will be able to design and build better robots than we can. That'll be the tipping point. We will merge with the machines, we will cheat death.'

'Machines can't love, though, can they?' I'd said, in hope more than anything. It prompted a smile from her I can still picture.

Neruda in the Woods

She was doing her thing with the trees. Securing a trio of screws to the bark of several small sycamores, their position on the trunk marked precisely by a moulded template he'd carried from the car. Satisfied each screw was at a perfect ninety degrees, she fixed the dendrometer to them, where it sat like some three-legged parasite.

'Why can't you just put a tape measure around it?' he said.

'Not accurate enough. This measures the growth to a hundredth of a millimetre.'

'It's all about girth with you lot.'

'Shut up and pass me the caps.'

He handed her three small plastic covers, their role to prevent passers-by gouging themselves on the screw heads, though it seemed few people ventured this far in to the woods. Finally she attached a numbered tag between the screws and recorded the tree's identity in a notebook.

It was unseasonably hot for late spring and he wished he'd worn shorts, despite Mia's warning of knee-high nettles and blood-lusting ticks. She was a year into an ecology PhD, studying the effects of climate change on temperate woodland, initially in the UK, and later, if funding permitted, in the forests of South America. This was her closest site to the flat they shared a mile from campus, yet still an hour's drive away, and he already regretted being marooned in the middle of nowhere with only a much-read Neruda for company.

'You can help me,' she'd said last night. 'Or get on with some work. We'll see a deer if we're lucky. You could put it in a poem again.'

He huffed but spared her his refrain of there being nothing original to say about nature.

His own part-time doctorate was faring less well, the title of which he could now hardly fathom, despite sharing his supervisor's enthusiasm when the two of them had conceived of it a year ago. As well as his thesis, he was tasked with the composition of an entire collection of poetry, an endeavour that would presumably overwhelm him were he to dwell on it.

Ostensibly he was here today to make Mia feel safe after the incident last week. Two men in their early twenties had approached her, asking the time in a way that meant it was of no consequence to them. She had been about 40 minutes' walk from the car and until then hadn't seen anybody all day. The one who did the talking had a faint stammer and for some reason Mia wondered at first if he was in the care of the other, the interaction part of some therapeutic strategy. He then asked what she was doing, again little interested in the response, despite it being the glamorous version, the one omitting long days in the rain, the equipment failing, her falling over or hitting a thumb with the hammer. After some unsubtle leering, the men left.

'It was just odd. They didn't have a dog or any good reason to be there.'

'Perhaps they were doing PhDs.'

'There was something feral in the eyes of the one who didn't speak, a sort of primitive calculation.'

Apparently, the first wolf whistle came a few minutes after they were out of sight, a strident burst that repeated every few minutes at various points around her. He'd suggested it was harmless, that men did it without thought, that while being puerile or degrading, it was never threatening.

'If I felt threatened, then it was. It's an instinctive thing; you wouldn't understand.'

'As a man.'

'Yes.'

She'd continued to work that day, every now and then checking whether her phone had a signal, which it didn't. When an hour later, having moved to a new site, she heard more noises – the crack of twigs too large to be an animal, and then more whistling – she pretended to call someone, announcing into the phone that she was on her way back.

'You were well-armed,' he'd said, several of Mia's tools being potentially lethal if wielded correctly.

It wasn't lost on him, how she left the flat each morning with an arsenal of gear most regarded the preserve of men: two types of hammer, a cordless drill, tool belt, two tripods – an entire car devoted to the creating and capturing of data. Returning before dark, hands and forearms scratched, a weal forming in one palm, she would ask how his day had been, what was for dinner.

'It makes me angry. Like I need another thing to consider, to factor in.'

'I could come with you,' he'd said, thinking it something he should say.

'Jesus, a chaperone. Has nothing changed?'

In the end they settled on his keeping her company the next few times, to take some reading with him, see if the men returned.

Mia was holding a Perspex square to the sky now, a length of string attached to it, the other end held to her face, to keep the distance constant, he supposed. He tried not to look or sound bored as he wrote down the values she called out to him, numbers that might one day form government policy or more likely be used to condemn one. There was something in her approach – to her degree, to life – that fitted well the demands of her subject: rigour, discipline, structure – qualities his creative self found alien. Science was something you did; it was unashamedly reductive. You plucked a theory from the air, then tried to disprove it. You made the complex simple, unlike art, which did the reverse. This didn't demean science's value, he liked to say to her in arguments, only its worth.

'I don't even know what you mean by that,' she would say. 'Or care.'

As far as he could tell, Mia came from a long line of distinguished academics, all of whom would no doubt be appalled at her choice of mate. Her father was a fellow of the Royal Society, while her great-grandfather, a brilliant mathematician and Oxford Blue, had a chess move named after him, setting the bar rather high for subsequent generations. By contrast he had fallen into a research degree in an attempt to stave off serious employment a little longer, a scholarship bestowed his way thanks largely to his cleverly anarchic pastiche of Kipling's 'If—' being placed in a national competition.

'I just don't think they understand what a creative writing PhD is,' Mia had said after taking him to meet her parents. 'They're old school. To them practice isn't research.'

And hidden somewhere among these words, he suspected, lay her own reproach of his vocation.

He watched as Mia attached red cable ties to scores of saplings. This achieved she fitted the fisheye lens to her camera, giving a hemispherical image of the canopy above. There were fewer nettles here, bluebells carpeting the ground around them, apparently native, which was prefer-able to their invasive Spanish counterparts. This was another cause trending in his girlfriend's realm, the resisting of non-native species, though it seemed there was debate about what constituted this, Mia's position taken at the point Britain separated from mainland Europe after the last Ice Age.

'Bloody grey squirrels,' he liked to say. 'Coming over here, taking our jobs, our women.'

They'd met as undergraduates at some hybrid event, an attempt to marry science and the arts, the cross-fertilisation appearing to have only modest success, with each faculty amassing at opposite ends of the room, politely disdainful of one another. What he and Mia lacked in the way of intrigue for each other's discipline, they made up for with a synchronicity in their visits to the bar. Upon their fourth convergence, he risked his best science joke.

'Why did Schrödinger work in a very small garage?'

'Go on,' she said jadedly though not entirely appalled at his presence.

'Because he was a quantum mechanic.'

There followed a largely tepid courtship as both lacked either the romantic ambition to afford the thing signifi-cant status, or to terminate it. He still fancied her, especially when they got drunk, which was less often these days, it being generally reserved for visits to Mia's parents, where the malts were single, the wine vintage, her father demonstrating each time the famous bishop sacrifice that had conferred eminence upon the family.

He looked at his phone, to confirm Mia's claim of their isolation.

'You'd think it possible to get a signal anywhere these days,' he said. 'I mean, if a drone can target a wedding table in the desert.'

'Please, not again.'

Politics, unless inextricably bound to climate change, bored her. It wasn't that she lacked compassion, more that other matters were trivial by comparison, which was hard to argue with at times.

'If there's no planet,' she would say, 'what does it matter how governments behave or who invades who?'

He'd pointed out there would always be a planet, at least until a swollen sun engulfed it. Just that it would be uninhabited.

'And what,' she said, 'would be the point in that?'

He helped her carry the gear to the next site, a cluster of mature beeches, their smooth, elephantine trunks rising to a denser canopy. Mia changed the drill bit to allow for the harder wood and began marking the bark. As he divided up the packed lunch, birdsong poured down on them with the overhead scramble for territory. He used to mine the natural world as an undergraduate, his verse tending towards the overwrought, the affected: light always *slanted,* air had to *shimmer.* Skies were *rinsed* of colour, frost *clung* to everything. The sea possessed a fury as it *roiled;* dusk *blunted* the day's hard edges. All of which made him nauseous now if he read it back. Not that Mia held undue sentiment for nature beyond a desire to be its custodian. At a recent dinner party hosted by a vegan couple whose company they enjoyed in small doses, she had announced that the best thing anyone could do for woodland conservation was to eat venison. Driving home they'd argued, as they invariably did when only one of them drank.

'That thing you always say in public,' she'd said, 'about there being more to life than books but not much more.' It was true he often said this, a nervous tic almost, and not an original line at that.

'It's obviously flippant,' he said.

'But it isn't, otherwise it wouldn't have any impact. You say it to belittle people who don't read.'

There followed a ranting monologue in which he must have uttered some awful things, as he awoke on the sofa the next day, some malevolent creature hammering inside his head. Later, by way of apology, he wrote her a poem in which eco-conscious deer became cannibals until the woodland returned to pre-Ice Age levels. Mia had smiled but it merely returned them to familiar ground.

'Perhaps you should write a novel, something that pays.'

'It doesn't really work like that.'

Which it didn't. Plot was abhorrent to him. Language was his thing. He simply didn't understand how things *happened*, how one event led to another in a seamless narrative arc, stray ends all neatly gathered. Plot burdened everything; it was a lumbering behemoth, encumbered by its own contrivance.

They ate in silence, the ham and cucumber sandwiches wilting a little from the heat. He thought about what would happen if the men did appear, whether his attendance would inflame rather than dowse their belligerence. Perhaps they were already present, observing from deep in the foliage, biding their time, sharpening their whatever. He could muster no comparison that gave insight into how it felt, this threat of sexual violence. Whenever he tried, it merely manifested in physical terms, as an assault, which of course it was. He just couldn't conceive of its extra dimension.

Perhaps he would disarm the men with a poem, like in that terrible novel, the recital pacifying them, converting them from would-be rapists to aesthetes. Or after some heroic resistance, he and Mia would limp from the treeline at dusk, barely alive, the incident lending itself to some future prizewinning prose.

The dog was on him before he saw it. For a second the pain coming from his forearm seemed abstract, as if witnessed rather than felt, the noise, the violence of the movements, too absurd to acknowledge. The animal, if not a banned breed, closely resembled the type featured heavily in the media several years ago – squat, muscular beasts whose appearance mirrored that of their owners. Despite the dog's small stature, it had little trouble flaying his arm from side to side like a soft toy, its teeth only prevented from meeting by the bone between them. Amid his own tortured cries and the animal's low growl, he tried to make out the sound of an owner calling it to heel, but there was nothing, so with his spare hand he half-punched, half-slapped the dog's head several times and for a moment the thing loosened its grip, only to clamp on slightly higher up his arm. Blood now pooled from the punctures of this first wound, mixing with the dog's saliva and smearing through the air in scarlet sprays each time he was shaken. Turning on his side he tried to use his feet as weapons, but the angles were all wrong, what leverage he could muster missing the target by some distance. In the few seconds since the attack began, he could hear that his screams had risen an octave or so, the pitch shifting from pitiable to something inhuman. Still he presumed it would cease abruptly, the dog yanked off, an apology issued, his injuries more superficial than they looked. But like a seasoned tug-o-war champion, the animal's claws were now dug into the ground, gaining traction as it savaged him further. Fixing his eyes on the dog's for the first time, he realised the thing was trained to see this through to the end, every instinct and impulse it possessed channelled into his expiry.

The pain was unbearable now – wasn't adrenaline supposed to make itself known in such times? – and whether through agony or fear or both, he sensed he was about to pass out, the edges of his vision blurring, sound skewing as it diminished. Perhaps this was a good thing, a state that mimicked death fooling the dog into releasing him. Or maybe the mauling would continue even then.

It struck him as such an ignoble way to die, absent of any consumptive episode or substance misuse associated with his calling, although it was just possible, given the rare nature of such a demise, that his modest body of work would gain acclaim beyond its worth. Can't be many poets, established or otherwise, mauled to death by a dog. At least he wouldn't have to endure Mia's father pushing the same chess piece around a board again, or referring to a wine as chewy.

The first yelp was muffled, almost incidental, but the second rivalled his own earlier shrieking. With force that he wouldn't have attributed to her, Mia again brought down the larger of the tripods on to the dog's back, the energy of which he felt through its jaws and up into his shoulder. For the first time he could now see some doubt in its eyes, a sense that attention was warranted elsewhere, that things had shifted, and with the next blow the dog let go of him, fleeing into the undergrowth with a series of whimpers. Sitting next to him, Mia inspected his wounds, before wiping the tripod dry.

*

The stitches would be in for a week or so, the nurse said as she finished dressing his arm. A tetanus booster may be required, depending how up to date he was, and some antibiotics would prevent infection. She asked him what he did for work, whether he needed a sick note.

Waiting for his prescription, he tried to read some of the Neruda one-handed, but his head fuzzed with painkillers. Mia offered to get them some coffee from the machine, suggesting they stop for something stronger on the way home once she'd collected her stuff from the woods.

'What if it's still there?' he said.

'I'll hit it again.'

He pictured the dog, its acceptance at having to abort the attack as Mia bludgeoned it. How the presence of pain, once great enough, overrode its compulsion for violence, the association between the two states made.

The anaesthetic in his arm was receding now, a fierce ache making itself known. He'd thought to tell the nurse that his arm, his hand, *was* his work, that its immobility was a great loss to literature, but as ever the words wouldn't come.

Blowhole

Dear Mrs Stanley

Forgive me for writing, specially after so long. I remember the papers saying how you got so many letters, from all over the world, total strangers getting in touch and all, as if your business was theirs. Folk is queer, as my Preston says. I used to think how that's the last thing you'd want, that each one must sound the same after a while. Did you ever write them back? I suppose that would just encourage more. Mind, I suppose we is strangers, having never met, but I've thought about you so much, specially in the last few years, how we'll always have this thing connecting us, that it feels like we know each other. Preston says we ain't allowed to make friends, least not the sort who come round your house or invite you over for the holidays. Acquaintances are one thing, he says. Everyone needs them, to get by. Once, I got talking to the woman who runs the youth

121

centre down the park here, and I got all warm in me tummy cos she was speaking like we'd grown up together or something. She made me a cup of tea and moaned about the kids being rude and stealing stuff, but I could tell she was fond of them really. It was just one of them nice moments, and I started thinking we could meet up and do stuff together, as couples, and I almost ran home to tell Preston about how lovely this woman was and how nice it would be to go out to one of them new places across town, get one of those fancy meals you see on the telly, then maybe see a film all together, not that I like many films, but going to the cinema is fun whatever you see, don't you think? But Preston said, You've got carried away with yourself, we don't need anyone else. Excitable is what he says I am. So now I walk a different way through the park.

I miss the town and all them people living there. Does old Cowley still run that shop in the market, the one with the little clowns that turn round on a pole? Like acrobats, they are. I used to watch them for ages as a kid, worrying they'd run out of battery or whatever made them go round. And Bobby's Fish and Chips, I bet that's still there, even though everyone knew he never washed his hands or changed the oil enough. Best scratchings ever, mind, if you didn't have enough for chips. Mam still lives there, down past the memorial, but I think my brother has moved out. I miss them so much but Preston says we can't ever go back, not even for a day, and so sometimes I ring her up and just listen to her voice until she hangs up. I think she knows it's me, cos once she cried and didn't hang up, and we were both just there, listening to each other's breathing for what seemed like hours, little sobs coming through the earpiece like she had a cold, and I wanted to tell her about our new lives here and ask her about the clowns. In summer I picture her in the garden, deadheading the roses, getting annoyed at the snails in her beds, but not wanting to hurt them. She used to put them in a jar and take them down to that bit of grass by the coal yard, and we used to tease her, saying they would crawl back, how they always remembered which garden they'd come from, no matter how far you took them, that they had little compasses in their heads. Sometimes my brother would go and retrieve them, and line them up by the back door just before she went outside in the morning, and we'd hear her scream as we ran to hide. Imagine that, a line of snails all staring up at you. When I first met Preston, he told me I should respect her more, which wasn't really something I'd heard a boy say before. He said mothers were the most important thing in the world, and that nothing would function without them. I was really worried, bringing him home with me that first time, even though Dad had run off years before and I knew Mam wouldn't be able to stop me seeing him. But they got on like a house on fire, chatting about this and that, how best to light the logs when they were damp, how to fix the upstairs tap what leaked, which Preston eventually did though it still leaked a bit cos although he knows about a lot of things, he isn't always good at doing them. He can be real charming when he wants, charm the pants off anyone, especially the women. Mam didn't even seem to notice how much older than me he was, or if she did she turned a blind eye. My brother never liked him, but then boys can get funny with each other, can't they.

I saw you on that documentary last week, the ten years on thing, and it brought it all back, as if it happened yesterday. You looked so much older, I mean more than how someone would after that long. Sorry, that sounds rude and all. I'm no spring chicken myself now, although Preston says I'm still more beautiful than any girl he's ever seen, which is why I'm not allowed to dress all tarty, as it gives men the wrong idea and then they think it's OK to come over and talk to me, try to buy me a drink. Only want one thing, he says, so best not to encourage them. When he's out nights catching rabbits or fishing, I go upstairs and open the box of clothes hidden under the bed, things I've bought in charity shops, real pretty stuff that some elegant women must have given them, a long open-backed dress, a silk scarf that I try to make look nice but it never sits round my neck right. I pretend we're going to a ball or some big party, where all our friends are drinking fancy wine and passing round trays with those small pastry things on, and couples are dancing or playing party games. I tie my hair up, put some make-up on and a few pieces of jewellery Preston let me keep, and I walk all sophisticated round the bedroom, pretending to talk to everyone, who all laugh at my jokes, which ain't really funny, but it don't matter cos we're all friends and nobody judges us.

You looked so tired on the telly, as if you needed a really long sleep. You still have the same dog, I see. Or is it a different one? We have a Jack Russell, which Preston takes out rabbiting. It bit me once, so I didn't feed it for several days. Not that I told Preston, he loves that animal more than anything. I want to get a cat, but it wouldn't last five minutes with those two. Did you have any more children? The man on the programme didn't say. I shouldn't ask, I suppose. Me and Preston don't have any. He says it's my fault, that my insides don't work properly, but how would he know? Perhaps he's the one what's broke. I get sad, knowing I won't be a mam. Sometimes I follow the pretty women along the seafront as they push their prams, making sure they don't see me looking, or if they do I pretend I'm one of them, tell them mine is at nursery, which if I say enough times I believe it myself. Sometimes they let me put my hand in the pram, where if I'm lucky I'll get a finger squeezed and a big gurgling smile, although one woman started shouting at me when I kept my hand there too long, and I tried to calm her down but there's no helping some folk. Did I say, we live by the sea now, one of them little terraced cottages with a pretty garden? Each year a bit more of the coast falls into the sea, so nobody can sell them now. Our landlord tried to put the rent up last year, but Preston stood firm, told him no one else would live here, what with the damp. It's the salty air apparently. If you walk out on the headland, it's like you're on an island, and there's this blowhole you can stand by at high tide, and if you're brave enough you look down in it until the last minute, the water explodes out and drenches you and your face tastes of the sea. Mostly though I just pick flowers along the path there. Apart from the wood burner, the house isn't heated, so we snuggle up under a blanket with the dog on us. In winter Preston takes the truck out nights, fills it up with logs from people's yards or from the pubs out on the moors. He got caught once, I think, cos the police came round, but nothing happened. I mean how do you prove a load of logs are someone else's? I tell him we should be grateful for what we've got, that we don't need to thieve stuff. I suppose everyone wants a little more than they have. He doesn't know I'm writing this, he'd probably get one of his rages on. He's better than he used to be, but when that red mist comes over him. The first time I seen his meanness was down by the allotments, you know, the ones off Cecil Street? Our Dad had one before he ran off, nothing fancy and not that he grew anything, just went there to get away from Mam. Used to just sit in his chair, watching the day go by. We used to go down there in the afternoons, when it was quiet, have a smoke and drink whatever Preston had taken from home. He told me he had something to show me that day. Like a present, I said. Yes, like a present. I was supposed to be in school still, but Preston said teachers had nothing to learn me that he couldn't. They wrote my Mam, but I think she just gave up in the end, short of marching me there and tying me to the desk, there was nothing could be done. I wish I had gone to classes a bit more though. There's a library few streets from here, a poster in the window saying free computer lessons, and I tell myself I'll go in and ask, and learn stuff about the world, so I can better myself and come home and impress Preston, but I never do. That sounds funny, don't it, impress Preston.

It was raining that day at the allotments, big fat drops like someone had torn a hole in the sky, and I remember slipping on the ground and Preston laughing at me, at the mud all up my trousers, and I laughed too but really I felt like crying, sat there in the mud, looking up at him as he grinned and swigged whisky. We walked down the paths, and every now and then Preston would jump onto a vegetable patch and start pulling up everything, potatoes and parsnips flying through the air, swedes he liked to play football with, onions which he'd throw at me. Sometimes there'd be shouting from across the other side and we'd have to run till my sides hurt and I couldn't breathe anymore and Preston would tease me, tell me he'd leave me behind one day, and that perhaps I wasn't cut out for the sort of life he had in mind for us, which apparently would involve a fair bit of running away. We walked to the far corner that day, where there were some sheds, and I could see he'd broken into one from the back, a hole just big enough for a small person to get through, which in those days he was. I was glad to get out of the rain, and Preston lit up a couple of cigarettes, passed me one and told me to sit down. Want some, he said passing the whisky, and I pretended to take a big mouthful, but didn't really, although the fumes alone made me cough, which he thought real funny. Watching him then, the rain dripping off his fringe, smoking hard like some film star, it was the first time I knew I really wanted him, and despite what happened I let him have me later that night, in my room, hoping my mam and brother were asleep. I remember wondering, apart from the pain, what all the fuss was about. Still wonder even now, if I'm honest, and I'd like to say it doesn't hurt like that first time, but sometimes it does. Afterwards, I cried a bit, told Preston I loved him, saying it beneath my breath so he couldn't hear, cos he don't like talk like that.

That day, in the shed, he picked up this hessian sack from the corner, its top tied with a boot lace, and placed it by my feet, the bag moving a little from inside like it had a will of its own. Open it, he said, and my heart pounded away like a good 'un and I didn't know whether to be excited or afraid. Go on, he said, it won't bite. The knot was tight but I got my nail in behind it until it loosened. There was this awful smell that made me gag, worse than the whisky, don't mind if I never smell it again in a 100 years. At first, cos the rain had made it dark, I couldn't tell what I was looking at. The cat stared up at me, real scared, and I wondered why it didn't try to get out, but then I saw its legs was all limp, and that it weren't well at all, and I thought how nice that Preston had rescued it, even though there probably wasn't medicine in the whole world that could fix it. Can we keep it? I said. Course we can't keep it, he said. It's a stray. Probably got fleas and all. Best we put it out of its misery. He picked the bag up, looking at me all the time, telling me to stop crying, which I didn't know I was. I hated the noise it made, or the lack of noise now I think about it, when he brought that spade down on it again and again, but I think it was the best thing to do, not that I could have done it. Later, after I'd let him have me, I wanted to ask about how its legs got all limp, where he found it, but I didn't. I guess meanness just gets passed down. Preston told me once his father used to make him take a bath before caning him, so his skin was softer.

Do you still see your husband? The telly said you ain't together no more, which made me sad. To go through all that and then to lose each other. It's weird, but I guess in some ways it keeps me and Preston together. It's not like there's anyone else we can turn to, or tell. I still love him. He was my first, so I've nothing to compare it to, but we're happy in our own way. He's had others, a couple since we met that he thinks I don't know about, and there's this girl two doors down that looks at him like she'd let him do anything, and I can tell he wants to. Will you have more children one day? Perhaps you're too old now, though I read somewhere about a woman in her fifties, which is a bit disgusting when you think about it.

I wish Preston had stopped after the cat, so we didn't have to move away. Sometimes I hope they'll find us, bring us back, even though it means never seeing Preston again, leaving our cottage behind, never looking down into the blowhole again or picking flowers on the cliff path. Would they let me see my mam and brother one last time, do you think? Preston says he'd go down fighting. Not built for prison, he says. Don't suppose I am neither. He isn't a bad person really, he just goes too far sometimes.

I should go now, pop this in the post before he gets home.

I wish you could write me back.

Susie

An Arrangement

It is one of those late summer evenings in England – heady and languid, the garden's drowsy scent marshalling in me nostalgia for the dozen or so Augusts we have spent here, seasons laid down deep in the brain's circuitry, more felt than known. Of droning bees, drunk on one of the colossal lavenders behind the old rockery, the day's heat subsiding yet still irrefutable. I picture the summerhouse – where swallows nest each year, where we would converge as afternoons lapsed, to imbibe each other's days – its exterior, I am told, in disrepair. And beyond this, quilted fields stitched with hedgerows of yellowing hawthorn, the sparrow-haunted rowan richly berried, fragrant walks that should have been more prized at the time. The radio said our summers will become wetter now, last winter's flooding commonplace as our climate enters a new phase, one we have cultivated, if the science is correct.

The low sunlight illuminating my wife's shoulder as she sits at her dressing table is somehow both mellow and scalpel-sharp, some trickery of the new medication, I suppose, which, whilst inhibiting some of the pain, distorts reality a few degrees. She is precise in her movements, a well-honed routine to enhance a beauty that was, she insists, late to flourish and which is only now perhaps beginning to wane. Men age so much better, she is prone to say accusingly, although perhaps there is altruism here, in case on some level I am still preoccupied with how handsome or otherwise I remain. I want to speak, to deny the reminiscing further indulgence, but the moment is paralysing me beyond my own body's regard for this. Not because of her imminent departure, a vignette that has occurred monthly for the past year; but there is something to be marvelled at in this dance we are able to perform (it would be simple for her to get ready in another room), as if my involvement, albeit one of mere observation, is somehow vital, consensual. Some months she even solicits my thoughts on a particular dress, a combination of jewellery I think works best, and I advise with due sincerity, delicate in my judgement, fulsome in praise. Perfume, though, is her realm alone, as if it speaks to a level of intimacy neither of us can tolerate, its selection seemingly flippant, a final flourish of decoration rather than the olfactory manipulation it aspires to be. Whether she imparts more scent than the times we dined out together is hard to say; perhaps further adornment takes place in the taxi, a courtesy extended to me, one of several that have formed unbidden.

'You can ask me anything and I will tell you,' she said at the start.

'I know.'

And I have been tempted. Not from a rising paranoia or raging jealousy. More that I fear hearing such detail would arouse me on some level, allow a vicarious lust to play out, despite myself. But I don't ask. As lovers in our thirties, I would have tore open any such rival, or at least threatened to, confronted him with animalistic fury before collapsing a tearful wreck. Such confrontation is beyond me now, but I sense no real desire for it. I am not so naïve to mistake this for some Zen-like enlightenment, or worse still a Sixties openness to communal loving. I always wondered how that played out in reality, un-adulterated by the rose-tinting of hindsight. Was everyone who partook accepting of such frivolous hedonism, the sharing of orifices and organs, or was homicidal behaviour only kept at bay narcotically?

'Are you OK?' she asks. 'You seem distant.'

'I was just thinking,' I lie. 'Do you regret not having children?'

This isn't a fair question and could be construed as my attempting to mar her evening.

'Oh, darling, we've spoken about this.'

'I know, but you might have changed your mind.'

We were trying, right up until I became ill, which I suppose was rather late in life, at least for her. Careers had consumed us, the time never right. And then when it was:

not enough blue lines in the little window. Tests showed no reason for our fallowness; it was simply a matter of perseverance, of sending enough seed swimming in the right direction. But the next batch of tests we endured – I endured – were of another order entirely.

'I'm content,' she says. 'I don't really think about it these days.'

Absent of all segue she speaks of the dinner awaiting me, cauliflower cheese, that she'll bring it in as she leaves. I make a joke about it being my turn to cook, but it's an old, well-worn line and goes unacknowledged.

'You've got your baclofen,' she says.

'Yes.'

'And you can take more naproxen at ten o'clock.'

'All two of them.'

Six months ago, when my mood found a new nadir, I began hoarding pills, with no more intent than to experience the sense of control it offered, some small reclamation of autonomy. Ever since she found them, their administration has been piously governed.

'You never ask me,' I say.

'What you want for dinner?'

'Whether I regret not having children.'

She sighs, a minute outbreath escaping.

'Can we talk about this when I get home?'

'Will that be before or after the sun is over the yardarm?'

I can't help myself. I don't even feel the level of spite

this implies; it's as if I want to try it on – being a shit – like a jumper.

'I can't cancel now. We agreed. If you don't want me to go, you have to give me a few days' notice. It's courteous.'

This word seems to me inappropriate, their arrangement requiring a more squalid lexicon.

'I want you to go,' I say.' I can sort myself out if you pass me some tissues.'

'Please don't be crude.'

It's true, I can just about still, yet the thought fills me with weariness, the exhaustion of the thing, my mind the only reasonable place for sex to occur these days, and then only from habit. In the early years of incapacity we continued to make love, content in its gesture however unsuccessful the deed itself. And later, when this became impossible, she would use her hand, whisper lewd contrivances that led more to despondency than climax. Abstaining came wordlessly, a relief to us both.

And so my emasculation was complete. A man, in any true sense of the word, no longer. Whilst hardly the athlete, it has always been the loss of physical more than cerebral activity that I've felt more keenly. Who'd have thought batting at ten or eleven, plus eight overs of regulation off-spin for the village side ranked higher in my sense of worth than an associate professorship? Nothing like total debilitation to furnish a little perspective.

The blurred vision came at the end of a stressful week, where rumoured redundancies became reality, our department likely to bear the brunt, and so the early symptoms were neatly aligned with events at work. Medicine, I have learned, is a patient creature, never rushing to judgement, content in the knowledge time will out. And so a series of hoops must be passed through, each one narrowing, each one ruling out potential, usually less condemning causes. None of this was helped by my mild but well-documented hypochondria, which in the end even I clung to. Tingling or numbness? Almost certainly nothing of concern, came the counsel. Fatigued? Aren't we all. Even the disturbed balance prompted only rudimentary scrutiny, blood tests, talk of an MRI. But after the first seizure a neurologist thought it prudent to tap my spine for some of its fluid, a joyous procedure, which suggested my body, far from suffering the slings and arrows of modern life, had in fact turned on itself. Later a new vocabulary evolved: bedsores, converted bathroom, managing expectations. And how many people experience cannabis for the first time in their forties?

My wife stands and checks herself in the mirror, turning ninety degrees left then right, a look of satisfaction rather than vanity.

'I'm sorry,' I say, and she crosses the room, kisses my forehead, the Chanel still young, yet to blend with her own scent.

'If you're awake when I get back, I can read to you if you like.'

We are tackling my favourite Márquez, all 450 pages,

most of which I won't remember, at least not this time round. But the essence of the book lingers in the suburbs of my mind, and so despite my attention wavering every few lines, there is still pleasure to be had. Pleasure especially in the sound of the words, my wife's voice a blend of honey and whisky, a balm no painkiller can rival. I wonder what texts the students have been given this term, what anodyne classics have been selected for their enrichment, novels chosen by committee to illustrate technique or theme, rather than to delight in. A couple of colleagues visited in the early days, bearing gifts and conversations that groaned with formula, office gossip their stock offering. Better off here, they would say, away from it all. Certainly I was accommodated for in those final days at work. Reasonable adjustments, as they're termed, were made as symptoms advanced: a parking space, pressure on fire doors eased, reduction of hours. I worked from home where possible. I knew all my work was re-marked, that I was just humoured in the end.

My wife moves the Márquez onto the bed, placing it in the space she will later fill, a promise of sorts. I smile, knowing the pills will render me beyond storytelling later tonight. In her absence I will listen to the radio, a surprising source of company that I've neglected most of my life. During the worst relapses, when mobility is nothing but fantasy, entire days can be built on the scheduling of programmes from around the world.

I try to remember the first occasion the matter of her

taking a lover came up. Curious verb that, more some-thing you associate with a hobby, the taking up of a pastime. Which lover would madam like to take? Have you browsed our online options? Just click Add to Cart when you're ready. I know nothing of him, no particulars beyond a handful of unsolicited revelations: age (around ours, a little older), profession (middle management), marital status (widowed). So he at least waited, I thought.

'Just tell me he doesn't play golf,' I said. I couldn't stand that.

They met at badminton, or yoga, I forget now. He knows the score, of course, knows our *situation*. Presum-ably they still interact at badminton or yoga, but dinner and its attendant *digestifs* are kept strictly to the second Friday of the month, the first couple of which remained platonic, if I read between the lines correctly. She used his name more, was how it started, the word registering sub-liminally until one day its utterance became frequent enough to jar. And then came the conversation, the one you never conceived of midway through your marriage vows or on honeymoon as you coiled and writhed and devoured one another. A mature tête-à-tête, one that addresses base needs, that purports to be pragmatic, but in itself is enough to crush you. There would be no question of anything else, we agreed. Our bond was beyond severing, half a lifetime's narrative to this footnote, this loveless frisson. Like servicing the car, it helped to regard it. I could request its cessation at any time, and yet I have begun to cherish the mornings after, when she lies by my side and silently strokes my face deep into the day. It's as if she returns in need of forgiving, though no such exchange takes place. And then it's done for another month and I can almost forget about it.

She brings in dinner, checks I'm OK to feed myself, which sometimes I'm not.

'My taxi's here,' she says, and now I think about it I can hear the rapid tolling of the diesel engine, this vessel of sin, transporter of goods. I wonder what the drivers think as they drop her off at the same restaurant each month, this woman who sports a wedding ring yet is always alone. Do they speak among themselves about this fare, about the house in the adjacent village they collect her from in the early hours?

'I will always have my phone on,' she once said, in reference to my physical rather than emotional needs. 'If you text I will come straight back. He understands this.'

Very good of him.

When sufficiently strong I like to revisit in my mind our first few years together, conjure as vividly as possible our trip to Tuscany, to the Lakes, moments within moments kept alive by their rehearsal, my senses fed sound and colour and smell, words re-enacted. Done well my mind can even trick itself, escape its cage for a few minutes. I remember the time I fell in love with her, the exact second as new lovers in our twenties. We'd taken a small cottage on the Gower, and out walking one morning came across a table of free-range eggs for sale, below which was an honesty box. We had no money, but the thought of cooking up those eggs for breakfast was all we could think about. I suggested we just take some, that worse crimes happen all the time, but she insisted we write an IOU note, posting it in the box. After we ate them she walked back the few miles to settle up.

My wife kisses my cheek, tells me not to get into any trouble while she's out.

'I plan to have an ASBO before you return,' I say.

She's almost at the bedroom door when I speak again, the words sounding so plaintive they disgust me.

'Eat with me tonight.'

She looks hard at me, gauging the words, my face, to assess if it's still part of the banter. I lower my head like a child asking to take a puppy home.

'Please.'

And we remain there in bloated silence, the spoils of a marriage charging the air between us, giving it voltage, and as I stare down at my stricken being I want to say I am still me, the same collection of particles and molecules and memories, still more than this shape-shifting abomination can ever reduce me to. I am more than the sum of my broken parts and I thought I could share you but I can't.

Instead I ask her if this year's swallows have left.

Undertow

He watched from an upstairs window as she entered the water. It was one of the few not boarded up, this side beyond reach of even the most competent stone-thrower. The room itself was empty these days, save the rocking chair, where on occasion he'd observe the cycle of the Atlantic as it pitched and tossed, the wading birds prospecting the strandline. He'd vowed last year to make something of it, return it to the handful of habitable rooms, but there was comfort found in its sparsity. He supposed it would have been one of the more expensive guest rooms, and he imagined their mother proudly opening the door for visitors, letting the panorama announce itself.

He was not beyond prospecting the line of wrack himself, a source of endless flotsam: wood for fuel or furniture; a pair of sunglasses he wore to this day. He'd found shoes, dolls, hot water bottles, skulls of various mammals – all curated by the waves after their immense journeys. Twice a day the sea bestowed him with gifts. Once a dead seal lay across the seaweed, half its head missing, flank corkscrewed open – a propeller most likely – and for days he watched the gulls pick it clean.

The light was receding fast and he had to adjust his position at the window to follow the woman, could see that she was up to her knees now. She might still turn back, he said to himself. There was no need to do anything yet.

He didn't recognise her as someone from the village, reckoned on her being mid-twenties or so, a holidaymaker perhaps, though it wasn't the season. She would presume the house empty, its tumbledown façade and weather-worn roof, its proximity to the cliff that suggested the sea would one day claim it, which it would. He'd always regarded land as unassailable, the changes it endured too small to witness, giving an illusion of permanence. But he knew the sea's furious power now, which he'd listen to at night as it dragged away a little more of the rock beneath him.

To live on the edge of things, he thought. The meeting of two worlds, a liminal porthole from known to unknown, as land gave way to leagues of nothing but ocean. Their mother liked to say the sea was answerable to no one, that even God was made impotent by its will.

The woman was deeper now. Almost to her waist. He looked to see if anyone else was present, a dog walker or a lover for whom this spectacle was intended, but if there was the dark had displaced them. There would be someone fishing further along, but their focus would be narrow, outward looking.

It was a test then, as everything these days was.

After surveying the horizon for an hour, she had climbed down a less sheer spot on the cliff, mislaying her footing a few times. At one point she seemed to lose her nerve, but climbing back up must have felt equally perilous, and a few minutes later she was on the beach. He'd watched as she crossed the shingle, limping a little, the gloaming shape of her less distinct by the second, and had he not known of her presence she might have been just another shadow. She'd paused at the water's edge and for a moment he thought the reality of the thing would dissuade her.

When she went in her stride had been purposeful and every few yards she fell, recovered and continued.

And then she was gone.

He tried to open the window, to get a better look at the woman, but it had long since sealed shut. Whether the undertow had taken her, or one of the small ridges that fell away, she was no longer there.

There was anger in him now. This was what happened in the world, people forced their business on you, drew you into their lives whether you wanted it or not. Even here, where he'd cocooned himself from the world, fashioned a life of sorts for his middle years.

He took the stairs three at a time, the dog getting under his feet, excited at the prospect of some event or other. He was halfway across the garden when he thought of the torch, but that would take another minute, which could be the difference. The dog was barking now, playing some game, trying to herd him, and he shouted it down.

There was enough light to see the shape of things if not the detail, and he kept a good pace, knowing by heart the path's course to the clifftop. He tried to remember today's high tide time, calculate what force he would be up against.

His route to the beach was more plummet than calculated descent, the gorse slowing his fall a little. He stood, sensed that any injuries were superficial. The sea was a hundred yards or so away, distinguished from the beach only by its fluctuating, by a thousand ever-shifting contours. There had been moonlight on previous evenings, but the cloud was dense tonight.

The water was cold, even to him, each stride less productive than the last. His boots were soon small anchors, his jeans already twice their weight as he lunged forwards. Once up to his midriff he stopped, tried to becalm his breathing, knew this to be important. He realised he had no idea where she was, that she could be fifty feet or more away.

He could hear the dog barking on the shore, and he called it to quieten, so he could listen for splashes. Less than two minutes, he reckoned he'd been. Even if she'd been under all that time, the low temperature might save her, force the blood to vital organs.

The cold was deep in him now, his body slowing as it tried to preserve itself. He removed his boots, thinking he should have taken everything off on the beach, that the extra time would have been worth it.

He called out several times, felt the immense scale of the water around him. A small wave broke on his back, enough to unbalance him and he took in some water, lost the direction of things for a moment. He had tried, he said to himself. You couldn't stop someone if they were determined.

She burst through the surface a few yards from him, arms flaying, taking big gulps of air before going under again. He pushed through the water in pathetic slow motion until the seabed fell away and he had to swim. There was nothing when he got to the spot, and he felt with his hands and legs for something solid, his muscles claggy like they were in mud, and he knew he'd be of no help soon.

His leg was stuck now, caught on something, his instinct to kick out, to release himself, but he realised she'd grabbed his ankle, and so he reached down. He held his breath and allowed himself to submerge a little, trying to find something of substance, but she was pulling him further down, further out.

He managed to surface again, could hear the yelp of the dog and he took some big gulps before plunging again, this time forcing his upper body over itself so that he could swim down to her. He found what he thought must be hair and looped an arm under hers, knowing it was a final effort, that there would be only one go.

He'd read about drowning, of those caught in riptides, the swell and heave of the sea underestimated, the cold sapping all strength from even the strongest. Of waves that pounded down on you like a ton of gravel until you had nothing left. Sometimes fighting it was a mistake, the battering and winding all the worse for it. Soon you couldn't tell up from down. Panic became resignation, the breath held as long as possible but eventually the body disobeyed the mind and breathed for you, the lungs flooding. Some spoke of euphoria, a painless passing to unconsciousness, but he wondered if this was always the case. Once reconciled to your fate, it was better to inhale deeply, to hasten it all.

It was anger that leavened the woman, anger that she was drowning them both, and he pulled her up until they were both afloat, their heads almost touching, undulating on the surface like buoys. He turned her a little, coiled a forearm around her neck and began the swim to shore. When he could stand he moved behind her, held her in both arms, collapsing on the shingle as the dog yelped and harried.

Even in the half-light he could see her skin was grey, that the water had claimed its colour. He opened her mouth, pushed two fingers in, but it felt clear. He placed an ear to her mouth but could hear nothing beyond the waves or the dog. Pinching her nose shut he cupped his mouth to hers and blew hard, waited two seconds, then blew again. He tried to see if her chest rose, and when he couldn't he felt her wrist for a pulse.

He knew to press hard on her chest, a 100 compressions a minute, stopping at 30 to blow into her again, and this time he sensed her chest rise. When she convulsed it wasn't to bring water up but to vomit. Turning her on her side he again forced his fingers into her mouth, scooping the remaining sick out. The dog, he realised, had ceased barking, the game something sinister now, something to fear, and he turned her on her back once again. The cloud had parted a little and, her face burnished in moonlight, he got a first real sense of what she looked like. Serenely beautiful were the words that came, a waterlogged beauty.

He was angry again, but different to in the water. Hers was an age when it was all felt so keenly and there seemed no way to go on. An age of absolutes. Pain you think impossible to live with.

He forced more of his air into her, hoping some of the oxygen found a way, and then sat back, exhausted.

Life was there still, he felt, vaporous and fragile but apparent. He went to continue the resuscitation when the water came, burbling out of her like a blocked drain. She choked and he eased her on her side again, smoothed her back, and the dog resumed its barking.

He pictured his boots on the seabed, barrelling out on the tide, and he mourned their loss.

Looking up at the house, he thought it possible. She

wouldn't be so heavy, even with wet clothes, and after another minute he hoisted her over his shoulder and trudged across the shingle.

The whisky seared, its warmth welcome. He worked out the order of things, decided she was OK while he changed his clothes and lit the fire. Even if he walked to the village, to the phone box, she needed caring for now. He had put a blanket over her, but her wet clothes needed to come off, it was just a fact. Her breathing was at least regular now, broken only by a steady cough, and he felt sure all the water had come up. When he'd first placed her on the sofa, she was still unconscious and for minute it seemed he'd lost her after all, her skin sickly blue, the hope he'd had on the beach diminished. What would he do then, he'd thought. But then she'd spluttered some more.

He tried to recall the signs of hypothermia, knew you could recover then relapse. Pneumonia was possible too. Brain damage. He removed the blanket and began taking off her jumper, pulling each arm down over her hands, working the thing up over her head as he tilted her forward. The shirt next, its buttons slipping easily through their holes. She seemed to rouse a little and he thought to stop, to explain what he was doing, but she drifted away again, between worlds. The shoes were harder, their laces tightly knotted by the water, his fingers too thick, nails bitten too short to get any purchase. He tried to remove a shoe as it was but these too had contracted. Leaning back he opened the drawer of the coffee table, felt around for the scissors, and cut each lace below the knot. He thought he might have to cut the jeans, but after initial resistance, they slid down.

He stood back, took in this unfamiliar sight the universe had brought him. Like flotsam. A quick calculation was all it took, to recall the last time he'd watched a woman sleep this close up. More than a decade, and he tried to remember what intimacy felt like but couldn't. It was as if the body forgot, more than the mind: the brain knew the choreography, its specifics, but not how it felt. There seemed little equivalent, where something else was denied – food, exercise, drink – and the concept of it vanished from your mind. Returning only at a sight like this. She was, he saw now, probably not even 20, more like 18, the age his daughter would be.

He told himself to stop thinking, to stay with the order of things.

The fire hadn't caught properly, so he worked on it until the flames bickered and he was sure it would sustain itself. He sidled the sofa nearer the heat, then started to remove her underwear. If she came round he would stop and apologise, hope she remembered what had occurred.

The pants were skimpy, a lurid pink, and they rolled down her legs until they were just a wet cord, a figure of eight. The bra was dark green, her breasts pushed unnaturally inwards by it. Rather than turn or lift her again, he felt behind her and unclasped it, waiting for her to stir but she didn't. Their faces so close, he could smell the whisky on his breath. He adjusted each arm in turn and removed the bra, tried to contain his thoughts. And then she was naked and something in him did remember an aspect of it all, how it felt. An ancient arousal.

He saw that her left ankle was swollen, probably sprained on the cliff, or turned over in the water. He would put some ice on it. He replaced the blanket and fetched a towel, drying sections of her hair gently, before propping her head up with a cushion.

The dog watched him as he crossed the room. He poured another whisky and drank this one slower, following in his mind the warmth as it spread within him. He reckoned on it being around eight, perhaps a little later, and he tried to remember what plans there had been for the evening, what jobs he'd been minded to attend.

The wood could last the night, if he was careful with it. He'd fetch more when it got light. Turning the armchair out a little, so he could see both the fire and the girl, he let himself fall into it, thinking that if she didn't need checking on he could happily sleep there until the morning.

He thought again about a phone call, at least to report it, but the fire and the whisky were like anvils on his shoulders, and it was all he could do just to watch her. There had been a line into the house for the first few years, disconnected when he couldn't pay the bill. It perhaps cost him work, not having one, but he managed. He would walk to the village first thing.

It was almost dark in the room when he woke, the fire aglow but silent. The lambent sweep from the lighthouse crossed the far wall in cadenced relief. He half-remembered and looked to the sofa, saw the shape of her, this selkie of the sea. She was groaning, delirious perhaps, and the noise had been something unfathomable in his dream. He remembered he hadn't got the ice for her ankle, and it took all he had to rise from the chair. He put a lamp on and felt her forehead, which was warm but not hot. When he came back from the kitchen she was awake.

He held out the ice, which he'd put in a sock.

'Your ankle,' he said.

She looked confused but not afraid.

'You were in the water,' he said.

He could see she was thinking about his words, like they were a riddle to be solved, and there was embarrassment in him now, for knowing her intention, for reminding her. She scanned the room and then herself, lifting the blanket a little.

'I had to take them off.' They were wet.

She seemed to accept this, but it was hard to know. He had never been able to tell a woman's thoughts, knew not to try. She pulled the blanket up to her chin, but without panic.

'Where am I?' she said.

Her accent had a trace of something hard on it, Russian perhaps.

'In the house on the cliff, along from where you climbed down.'

She turned on to her side and winced, touching her ankle while trying to keep the blanket in place.

'I don't think it's broken,' he said. 'Sprained, most likely. I have some painkillers. And this.' He held out the sock again.

Kneeling at the end of the sofa he asked if she minded and she shook her head. The swelling was no worse than before and he held the ice there while she watched.

'Can I have some water?' she said.

He gestured that the ice was more important.

'I can hold it in place with my other leg.'

He left and came back with a filled pint glass and she drank hungrily.

'Try to sip it,' he said.

He put the box of pills where she could reach them, realised the folly of this, and eased two out from a strip.

He wondered what time it was, how long he'd slept.

'Are you hungry?' he asked.

She shook her head but then seemed to think about it some more.

'A little.'

'There's some stew.'

In the kitchen he saw it was 1am. The tide was up and he could hear its rhythmic roar, the crash each wave made, the guttural growl as it turned back on itself, raking the shingle. He remembered his boots, how well they fitted, the years they had left in them.

It had been so long since someone else had been in the house, and then not at night, and he didn't know what to think of it. He hadn't felt hungry until he smelt the food, the microwave turning the portion he'd left for himself last night. He tore some bread off, took it in, the dog eyeing him.

Passing the food to her, he saw that it didn't work, the mechanics of it.

'Have you some clothes I can borrow?' she said. 'So I can sit up.'

He left the food on the coffee table and went up to the bedroom, found the smallest shirt and jumper he had. Downstairs, after handing them to her, he hung her wet clothes on the back of two chairs, turning them to the fire, and left her alone. He took some cheese from the fridge, put it on the last of the bread and sat down.

He wondered how long he should stay out here, reckoned a few minutes to be sure. It occurred to him that the kitchen was a mess, more than normal, and after eating the bread he put some things away, filled the bin. He thought to put the radio on, to fill the silences, but knew the signal would be weak this time of day. There'd been a television once, though he'd not replaced it when it had broken.

Outside the living room he coughed to announce

himself. With a little effort the fire returned and he stacked a couple of logs in its centre, the dog replacing him as he stood.

'What sort of dog is that?' the girl asked.

'A lurcher, with a bit of something else.'

She looked confused and he thought of the word mongrel, but figured on her not knowing it.

'Cross-breed,' he said and she nodded.

He saw that she'd eaten some of the food and now gripped the water in both hands. She looked odd, sitting up in his clothes, and he had to check whether he was dreaming, decided there was too much continuity for this.

'Do you want me to call anyone?' he said. 'There's no phone, but I can walk to one.'

She shook her head and he thought there was perhaps fear in her eyes for the first time. He'd assumed there would be someone, despite her intentions.

'No one in the village?' he said.

'I don't live here.'

'The person you're staying with then?'

Another shake of the head. So far he'd only thought about her physical condition, what damage being in the water might have done.

'I can call a doctor in the morning.'

'My ankle?'

'Your ankle will heal. I thought someone to talk to.'

Shame bloomed in her and he wanted to take it back.

'But, yes,' he said. 'A real doctor, to make sure you're OK. Are you in any pain, apart from your ankle?'

She said that she wasn't, but that she felt weak.

He sat back in the chair and felt the fatigue everywhere, as if some vast gravity was at work, could feel his body, his hair, rimed with salt and sand. He tried to think clearly, about what day it was, what tomorrow held. He was due at the yard early, a big order to fill this week. It was all cash in hand, and nothing if you weren't there. Brutal work, it was, especially in the summer, though he didn't know from one month to the next when he'd be needed. The other two were brothers, their father the yard's owner, so he was only brought in for bigger orders. Between jobs he would go to the village once a week, ring the owner to ask if there was anything.

When not at the yard he maintained a few of the boats in the harbour, men he'd got to know from fishing, from the pub where he sometimes went. Men with sea in their blood, for whom life on land was never entirely trusted, true solitude found only on the water, where a living could still just about be eked out. Hardship etched in every feature; skin inked not in adornment, as it was these days, but from pragmatism, such artwork often the only way to identify a water-dwelling corpse. And their ancestors, sailors who had an image of Christ tattooed on their backs to deter the first mate taking the whip to them.

Payment for his work – mending nets, painting a hull,

removing algae – came with guarded civility, as if he had more in common with these modern fishermen. An outsider, from the family who arrived with lavish plans. They paid him with cash, a few pints, allowed him to occupy the fringes of their revelry after a good catch, sea shanties filling the night.

He had been told, as every newcomer who frequented the pub had, of the plague visited upon the village in the 17th century, carried by fleas brought in on cloth from London. In an act of selflessness, the village entered a lockdown, nothing coming in or going out until the epidemic had passed. A year later and more than half its population had succumbed, names writ large in the church. Supplies were still needed, so an exchange site on the outskirts was created, goods left one week, payment in sterilised coins the next. Such solidarity was not diminished by time.

Less edifying tales were also told, of the coast still possessed by the wraiths of wreckers, folk who profited from a place of serrated reefs and busy shipping routes, the luring of storm-ailed vessels to their demise an industry of its time. And the smugglers, rejecting of the duty imposed upon them, shifting contraband through labyrinthine tunnels, supplying a complicit community. You did what you had to.

He should like one day to earn a proper living, to know what was coming in. To buy a boat of his own, run trips to the island or get some lobster pots. Bend the world a little to his own will. There had been a small skiff when he first moved back, abandoned on the beach below, and he'd hauled it up one winter, worked on it in the outbuilding, and the project sustained him, gave him purpose. Once seaworthy he liked to row it out early or late in the day, like some crepuscular thing, the ocean his alone, and he would tie a baited line to the rowlock, sit back and watch the house as it lost or gained form. He rarely caught anything this way, was content not to, but to somehow be bound to the first humans to fish.

The girl was examining the painkillers.

'Take them,' he said. 'And then no more for four hours.'

He realised his own head hurt, knew he couldn't afford to get ill.

'You can stay here tonight,' he said. 'If you've nowhere to go.' He hadn't planned to say this, the words a surprise.

'Will your wife mind?'

He looked at the dog. 'It's just us,' he said. If she felt threatened by the absence of someone else, she hid it well.

'I always wanted a dog,' she said. 'As a child. Our mother said they take too much looking after.'

'She's no trouble.'

'My friend had one, but it was taken by a bear.'

He looked nonplussed at her, wondered if her brain had gone too long without oxygen.

'In Romania we have lots of bears. It smashed through

three doors to get to it, carried the dog off to the woods. My friend heard the cries for 10 minutes.'

His mind formed the image, found it both gruesome and comical.

'Do they ever take people?' he said.

'Just the tourists. If you go up in the mountains, you enter the food chain, and not at the top. They are fast, faster than people. At least if you are with someone, you only have to outrun them.'

He took a moment to get it, enjoyed the humour of it.

There was the silence again and he tried to think what to say. Upstairs he'd wondered what he should bring her to wear on her bottom half, but could think of nothing, so brought down a towel for her to wrap around.

It felt strange to feel responsible for something beyond himself, beyond the dog, even if only for the night. There was something natural in him that kicked in, and he thought, yes, everyone must have this capacity, but then he thought of men he'd met who hadn't. Who were built otherwise. And then he remembered that once he wasn't so different from those men.

'The fire should last now,' he said. 'You should try to sleep. I'll check on you later.'

He called the dog, but it ignored him and so he let it stay.

It was light outside, an hour or so past dawn, he reckoned, and he cursed. He should already be at the yard, and would be down a morning's pay even if he left now. Beyond the garden, out over the cliff, a pair of fulmars rose from the sea fret and tacked into the south-westerly. His limbs were heavy, like he'd spent a night out on the boat, and then he remembered, checked with himself it had happened.

When sleep had come, it was riven with images of his time inside, when all you could do was shut yourself down, like a hibernation, but one you remained primed in. Each time he woke, he had checked on the girl, reconfigured the blanket, made sure her ankle was raised. She'd removed his jumper and had both arms stretched outwards, as if she were poised to dive off the sofa. He felt her head again, tried not to wake her. By the second or third time, the fire had burned out and he left it, the dog following him upstairs.

He thought this morning how easy it would've been to have ignored her, mind his business. To hear a week later of a body washed ashore in the next cove, to read who she was in the paper. There was a time when he'd have felt nothing, watching her submerge and not surface, and it troubled him that this was no longer the case. A man he'd once shared a cell with drew a bladed tooth-brush into another's cheek and he had felt nothing at the sight. A mouth made twice its size. It was just an event, this laceration of the flesh, like any other thing that happened. Yet the girl's situation, despite it being of her choosing, had given rise to something else and he had risked his life for it. Not that she had seemed grateful. And perhaps on recovering she would simply repeat her efforts, his actions only prolonging her misery.

He heard the girl in the hall. She was working her way along the wall, trying not to put weight on her ankle. She'd put on her trousers, though he could see they were still damp. His jumper looked even bigger on her this morning, the arms traipsing like a straitjacket.

'I need to pee,' she said.

He looked up the stairs, but said nothing. She gave out a huff, sat on the bottom stair and worked her way up backwards.

'Would you like some breakfast?' he said, but her attention was on the stairs and their negotiation.

He needed to make a decision about work. The girl seemed in no hurry to leave – owing mostly to her ankle, he supposed – or to contact anyone, and despite there being little of value in the house, he had no desire to leave a stranger alone here for any time. He would walk to the village and call the yard, say he was ill. There would be no sympathy, only a reminder that others could replace him if he made a habit of it. If the girl left soon, he'd go in this afternoon.

He heard the bathroom door shut.

'I'm taking the dog out', he called up.

After making the call, he went back to the house, but continued along the path past it, to give the dog more of a run, to collect his thoughts. The owner of the yard had merely said tomorrow, and he knew what was meant by this. There was no recourse, no debating it: an employer who asked no questions – who cared nothing for your past – held no obligations towards you.

The dog had something's scent now and lagged behind. He looked back at the house and for a moment was fifteen again, oblivious to the true savagery of life, thinking that some glorious future awaited once the tumult of youth had been navigated. He recalled coming here on family holidays, before they moved down, their father taking them rock pooling, exploring miniature shape-shifting worlds, microscopic life amid tendrils of seaweed, scrambling over lichened rocks, the house on the cliff something that caught their eye even then.

He could see how nearer the cliff edge it was after three decades of erosion, waves tireless in their undermining, water channelling its way along faults in the rock, later expanding as ice, rupturing from within. The house would never sell again, the subsidence irreversible. Ten years, the structural engineer had told him after his mother's funeral, perhaps a little more. They could lay grids of steel tendons over the cliff-face, calcify with concrete where possible. The cost, though, would be his alone, the local authority prepared to bolster the base with boulders, but little else.

There was an offer – enough to do something with, perhaps even to buy a caravan up the coast – a firm building apartments for affluent surfers, second homes for business types, sky-stealing grotesques. The coast as a playground. They'd expanded either side of the village in the last few years and had a plot directly behind the house, two fields back. He hadn't understood at first, why they offered anything at all, realising later that week they would raze it to the ground, this blight that affronted the view. He'd given it serious thought, for there would be no insurance when the first bricks joined the beach, no relocation by the local authority. But the harder the company pushed, the more resistance he felt, the fight something to sustain him. Letters still came every month or so, but he'd stopped opening them.

He called to the dog and this time it came, passing him, stopping to drink from one of the rivulets, and he chased it on, in case something's carcass lay upstream. Few rivers went quietly to their end, and he liked how they overshot the cliff edge here, announcing to the sea their return, water's great migratory cycle, always finding its way, returning to itself. And the waves surging in to unite with the fresh water, their advance a mathematical artillery, as was everything in nature, patterns repeating. Spits and dunes formed this way, subject to the earliest laws.

The fret had cleared now and he could see out to the island, its silhouette from this angle a leviathan rising through the water, its lithe body segmented, head turning unflinchingly inland. It was all that was left of the old land, a reminder that the sea always triumphed in this incessant struggle, millennia of resistance by the land undone, only this granite outcrop enduring. Its stone walls built by convicts bound for the Antipodes, hived off in secret.

He scanned the beach below, harbouring a fantasy that his boots might lie undamaged somewhere along the tideline and not a mile or more apart, sidling like crabs on the seabed. Remembering his efforts of last night a great fatigue gathered in him, and he headed back to the house.

The girl was in the kitchen when he got back.

'You should keep your ankle up,' he said.

She hobbled from one cupboard to the next, shifting cans and jars about. Her hair had braided itself from the salt and sand of last night, her smell nautical, like when the dog went in the sea. Her nails were mostly bitten down, a residue of varnish garnishing them, and whereas carrying her from the beach he'd thought her slight, she looked strong in the kitchen's half-light. He watched her move from one end to the other, remembered the feel of her skin, warmth from the fire in it.

'Do you not eat food?' she said.

She picked up a near-empty bag of pasta, inspected then dismissed it. He supposed food wasn't a priority for him, more something that either happened or didn't. He caught fish most weeks, went to the village shop now and then. Purple laver could be harvested when he wasn't carrying back driftwood. They got pasties at the yard sometimes. As long as the dog didn't go without.

169

The girl moved to the window, seemed transfixed by the pewtered sea, the light ghosting across it, and he recalled his mother standing in the same spot, watching for hours the Atlantic's endless nothingness, it somehow both inert and active. Something to be revered.

He fetched wood for later. Outside, the day had got up into a frenzy. It was a house built on a tapestry of sound: a dozen different winds, waves that growled and pummelled. The *rark* of gulls and the *seep seep* of their young. And underscoring this, the sea's white noise, coming without beginning or end from its machinery.

When silence finally came, in the fragile spaces nature afforded it, it discomfited him, drew attention to his thoughts, to the things missing in a life. A wife and daughter. Where were they now? Abroad, he had last heard. There had been cards once, from his daughter at least, formal, alluding to little. And she had written to him in prison, and he'd slept with the letter beneath his pillow. It was in those years, before arriving here, that he truly learned what despair was.

Autumn, having clung on as long as it could, now lapsed, its fragile, mellow light rinsed from the landscape a little more each day, replaced by something harsher. He tried to picture the garden in that other time, but couldn't, remembering only a couple of weather-beaten benches corroding in the spumes of brine. He'd had plans for it after their mother died: a vegetable plot, a new stone wall to protect it from the Atlantic's barrage. Now overrun with weeds, it served well as the dog's toilet, the far side used occasionally by fly tippers, piles of rubbish he'd allow to accumulate until it threatened the beach below.

The tide was approaching, liver-hued in the mid-distance, awaiting its lunar calling. Membranes of wrack bisected the shingle, desiccating in the wind. A solitary figure a hundred yards out, digging for lugworm, and he could almost hear the slurp of mud as it was excavated. And beyond the figure, listing in sepulchral permanence, the wreck of an old herring boat, all paint peeled from its timber, its wheelhouse salt-eaten, hull heavily barnacled. To the west the island, little more than a snarl on the horizon, the sky above leached of colour. He walked across the garden to the cliff edge, its base benign in the sea's absence, respite from the twice-daily union, and it was hard to imagine rock being undone by water, as if the land was exposed flesh, the sea a scalpel. The clan of wind turbines, so long a source of antagonism for the village, a benign apparition to the east. It was easy to trick the eye on such days, to render the sea two- rather than three-dimensional, its horizon a height instead of a depth, a wall of water, amassing like some invader.

Looking up to the window, he took some comfort at the girl's presence, this good thing that he had done, knew that soon – later today, tomorrow – he would come back to the house, from the yard, from a walk, and she would be gone.

Lucca: Last Days of a Marriage

Even mid-morning the heat is the wrong side of toler-able. An ambient ferocity that consigns him to torpor between short bursts of activity, the discrete parts of the day bound by the searing onslaught. He'd left the hotel an hour ago, the *wap wap* of the room's fan still occupying like rotor blades some frontier of his mind. He starts, as Pollex's characters had, encircling the town along its walled walkway, stopping at each bastion, grateful for the leafy shade on offer. He felt the narrative ambled at this point, became part-travel guide as it documented how the wall was designed by Leonardo, how each of its four sides was given over to a different species of tree. The stone-work, an actual guidebook informs him, acts today as a liminal boundary, dividing ancient from modern, contem-porary life held at bay where possible. Pollex reminds readers the town had once rivalled Florence for promi-nence, that Caesar himself visited, Dante too while in exile. He could, of course, now edit such detail, mute the verbiage to his own satisfaction, the only reins a ghostly voice he is obliged to hear.

A young couple kiss against a centuries-old trunk, incautious, solipsistic. From their lack of wilting he figures them locals, Tuscans for whom the heat is a frivolous matter, who know nothing of wet Tuesday mornings on the M25. He imagines what it would take to interrupt them, what measure of sound or force would untwine the pair, remembers on some level the exhilaration they are feeling. It's not that he begrudges them exactly; more that he wishes to point out love's inexorable arc.

He removes his hat, fans himself before walking on. On waking he had been surprised at the absence of a hangover, and the assessment had indeed been premature, the sun now drawing it from deep in him and for a moment he thinks he might be sick. *Cretino!*

A waft of sweet *buccellato* arrives from below, and after pretending to himself that he is hungry, he takes the next set of steps down into the old town.

His task, he supposes, is an unusual one, though literature boasts its share of posthumous publications, books part-finished, part-edited upon the author's demise. That Pollex set much of the novel in Tuscany was, initially, a source of delight on learning he would be required to visit, to immerse himself in the region's underbelly, let *la terra* permeate him. Much of the book's closing chapters take the form of notes, and so it was deemed necessary to work on it *in situ*, to strive for a resonant denouement. But the undertaking has now become burdensome, not least because Pollex's characters were witnessing a marital collapse to mirror his own.

He'd worked with Pollex for the first couple of novels, books that sold in moderate number, establishing the man as a seasoned mid-lister, unremarkable yet in possession of a steady and loyal readership. His own poor health had seen a parting of ways for the next work, a colleague stepping in, presiding over what turned out to be Pollex's 'breakthrough' book, a genre-bending tale set in post-apocalyptic Glasgow that bore no resemblance to the lyrical realism preceding it. Had it been a debut, nobody would have touched it, least of all his own publishing house; they were simply honouring a contract, assembling a novel they suspected wouldn't sell.

But sell it did. Despite an age of endless, readily available analysis, nobody really knows why a book does well: a series of favourable reviews, celebrity book clubs, influential bloggers – all play their part, but guarantee nothing. Word of mouth is still the overarching factor, and how do you measure that? Within two months of publication, Pollex was the author everyone wanted to interview, to pastiche. The rights sold in thirteen territories, film options arrived soon after. Some of the parties are, he suspects, still going on now.

So it was a surprise when they asked him to return to edit *Lucca*, the locum colleague jettisoned at the author's request. From the early drafts, however, it was clearly going to be a difficult book: not at all the anticipated sequel in terms of style or content; more a return to his earlier *oeuvre* but with even less commercial appeal. As the book's editor he was frequently drawn in meetings to comment on its plot, its formula – its comparisons to The Previous One – and he'd searched hard for a balance between cryptic and tantalising. In truth it was obvious Pollex regarded his departure an artistic compromise too far, despite the economic freedom it bestowed him with. It was as if he was saying, Look I can write a bestseller if I want to. Now let me return to the real stuff.

The sun is directly overhead now, chromic and irrefutable. He needs to find a café, sit in shade and rehydrate. Later, when it is cooler, he will drive up into the hills to the north, navigate the serpentine road into the Apuan Alps, where the marble Michelangelo himself once quarried renders the great slopes as if snow-clad. Then, if he's not too tired, on to the verdant valleys of Garfagnana. Pollex mentions the region several times, though his characters are too preoccupied by hostilities to visit, its treatment in the book providing, he senses, excessive adornment, self-congratulatory prose. And yet he is drawn to the place simply from Pollex's vicarious descriptions, a Shangri-La where, apparently, the silence is absolute, the terrain timeless. He told Pollex on more than one occasion that the allegory of the couple not making it to the hills was strained, that why describe it all if no action takes place there. But as with other counsel he offered during their early editorial exchanges, the sales of *Lucca*'s predecessor allowed Pollex to resist.

He takes a long drink from a fountain in the piazza, the water rarefied, seemingly ancient, and he imagines it cleansing him of toxins and memories, imagines remaining under its flow for the rest of the day. It is only when his stomach swells in discomfort and he senses an audience that he withdraws his head and converges on a nearby café.

He orders a coffee in Italian, the waiter responding in English. What is it they pick up on? The attire, the accent, the general unease in posture? And why English? Couldn't he be Dutch or Finnish or Israeli? He once quizzed a taxi driver on the matter the only other time he'd visited the country.

You English are so polite, the man had said. An Italian would be on his phone, telling someone where and what he ate last night, which restaurant he was going to this evening. But mostly it's the shoes. You wear such bad shoes.

Vero.

When his wife left last year – a sudden though not unexpected departure – his physical appearance became a source of concern for the first time in a decade, the separation ushering in a mid-life crisis of sorts. Scrutiny revealed tufts of errant hair accumulating from his nostrils and ears, a stomach that bore testimony to endless lunches with authors – a culture of indulgence despite the suspicion people were about to stop buying books. His wardrobe, he realised, boasted a spectrum of beiges and browns, most of it bought more than five years ago. His hair, once profuse and lustrous, had long ago begun the retreat crown-ward.

He joined the gym, vowed to cycle to work. Researched what was fashionable, purchased some clothes he suspected would remain unworn. In the end he settled for having his teeth whitened, a procedure that served only to draw attention to the weathering of his other features. *Grande cretino!*

Is there someone else, he had asked her as she packed that day, and he could see that there was.

He considers buying a paper, if only to parade it to the waiter when he returns, but such haughtiness is beyond him today. Instead he sits back, adjusts the chair to be in consistent shade. Above him, perhaps two floors up, there is some kind of commotion, an instant in which the natural order of things is displaced, and he looks up at the blaze of colour alighting from the wall. The departing jay, he realises, has a gecko writhing between its talons, the bird rising in near silence into the thermals. He looks around but is the only witness to this remarkable yet trivial spectacle. A few moments later the jay is little more than a speck over one of the town's churches, and then, despite the unbroken blue canopy, there is nothing.

Such a demise has its appeal, he thinks, swift and efficient, a final journey above all you have inhabited, the lizard oblivious on all but the most primal level to what was playing out, its brain eliciting a flush of chemicals to evoke fear, before ... what? Resignation? Nothing? For his own amusement he bestows the gecko with superior cognisance, imagines it thinking: this is something that hasn't happened before. Of it being thrilled by this novel vantage point.

The waiter places his coffee down wordlessly, attends to another table. The absence of insincere small talk found in other countries is, he has discovered, refreshing, allowing him to fully attend to the melancholy. Pollex's couple had been here a little later in the year, when the town was immersed in its month of celebrations, the climax of which is the procession of the Holy Cross, a pageant that departs from San Frediano Basilica, a trail of *lumini*, a thousand candles and lamps snaking through the town to the cathedral. Again the symbolism is clumsy, Pollex using the parade to signify the journey his characters are on, the lights, on reaching the Duomo, finally extinguished.

The coffee, as ever, is good and he senses his hangover receding a little, vows to take up smoking again. He watches a middle-aged couple loiter in front of the Basilica, perhaps on the cusp of an argument. The standoff is broken, their ensuing embrace an extended one. Above them is a golden mosaic, an enthroned Christ and, after counting them, he supposes the apostles. He wonders if Pollex's frequent references to religion represented something beyond character introspection, that somewhere beneath the surface prose lay clues to the author's fracturing mind.

He leaves some coins on the saucer. As young lovers in Paris, they had once fled from a bistro without paying. It wasn't planned, but they had little money and the food had been ordinary, the service lacklustre and, at times, rude. He'd assumed she was joking, but the moment, fuelled by the bottle of red they'd shared, gained a silent traction, and before he knew it they were shuffling towards the door, giddy with the thrill of the thing, feeding off each other's daring. They assumed nobody would notice, imagined a gradual realisation at the end of the evening, the English couple who'd had cassoulet and shared dessert. An acceptable loss. But they were barely a 100 yards away when one of the larger waiters burst from the door behind them, shouting, running, brandishing something. He'd wanted to turn back, announce it was all a prank, but instead they ran and ran, finally finding succour in a crowded bar where they removed their jackets, melted in to the gloaming with a large group of musicians. They'd sensed the man occupying for a while the fringes of the room, but their cover proved adequate. He never told her how afraid he'd been.

He crosses the square, stops to watch a puppet show

with a dozen others. He is in no hurry, Lucca – the ancient Lucca – one of the few cities to permit this. He cuts through the lattice of medieval streets, imagines Pollex imagining his characters, manipulating them to his aesthetic end. Occasional fissures between buildings afford a glimpse of the tree-topped Guinigi Tower, the town's totemic landmark, its lofty garden of oaks incongruous amid the firmament. He should climb the steps, count them as she tended to all considerable staircases, childlike in her tallying. Often, if descent failed to match in total accent, she would negotiate them again.

Did he know even then that he was only borrowing her? If he had, he chose to ignore it, ignore the sand as it fell through their hourglass. The someone else turned out to be a colleague, encountered on a research trip to Mexico; he hadn't wanted the details but she'd told him anyway. Old love rendered ordinary by new.

He emerges into a smaller square, a large poster boasting a Bob Dylan concert (though closer inspection reveals the date has passed), another reminding visitors that Puccini was born here. Below them a father and daughter set up a keyboard and amplifier, test the volume, the girl placing a soft hat on the ground. He thinks to listen for a while, sit somewhere, order a *bicchierino* of grappa. Instead he follows the signs to the botanical garden, judges it to be somewhere he can make notes on the manuscript.

The garden, a triangular plot in the south-east corner

of the town, turns out to be small, the woman taking his money keen to point out that, despite its size, they still have more than 200 species of plant. A pair of sculptured lions guard the gate above her, and he imagines Pollex admiring them. Inside there is a series of large ceramic medallions illustrating milestones in the garden's history, such as the planting of its prized Lebanon cedar in 1822. He locates the giant tree, stands beneath it, tries but fails to contemplate such longevity, its silent majesty commanding veneration. It is older than *War and Peace*, than *Moby Dick*, and he understands, now that it is too late, her affection for the natural world. On the grass beyond the tree, a small boy is trying to assemble some sort of glider, the child's face scrutinising the parts, as if not knowing where to start. He thinks to walk over, squat down and help, but deems this a source of potential disquiet in today's climate, the gesture doubted. Instead he finds a bench in some shade, takes out the parts of the book he has brought.

It was three days before anyone found Pollex, the garage not thought to be in use. The absence of a note seemed odd at first, a man who'd spent his life curating words, strangely silent. There had been a will, instruction left for the work-in-progress to be edited before publication, suggesting he'd intended to complete it first. To those on the outside there had been few if any signs. Rumours circulated, of a writer who sensed his creative well had run dry, who realised *Lucca* would be mauled by critics. He wrote to Pollex's widow, offered commiserations to her and their children. She replied, declining the offer to have any input into the novel, remarking that she was sure he'd do a fine job.

He thinks of how he will tie up the loose ends, wonders what Pollex had in store for his couple; there seemed little prospect of reconciliation, and yet he is tempted to leave open the possibility. Pollex's agent was equally unaware of the man's state of mind, could shed no light on what path the final few chapters should take. As for the earlier sections, he'd apply the same process he would to a finished work, asking only, can the book live without this? Regardless of how strong the writing was, how beautiful or poignant or insightful, if the answer was in the affirmative, it was culled.

Despite their working relationship – almost a decade if you discounted the two-year forced sabbatical – he had only actually met Pollex a handful of times. As writers went he was the usual mix of awkward outsider and engaging conversationalist, part romantic, part pragmatist. He came late to words, at least in terms of fiction, had lived several lives before early redundancy from a teaching post forced a replotting of the vocational odyssey. What struck him most when he first read Pollex was that he could write, really write; so many books he edited were conceptually and structurally and tonally strong, would sell in significant number, but which neglected the music of a sentence, its ability to be affective rather than merely expository. Abstract instead of just literal. Pollex, he felt, *troubled* his sentences into existence, cared for them as one might a prized possession, or one's child. He was a stylist who, until *Lucca* at any rate, knew when to get out of a sentence, knew when lyricism became onanism. The editor's role, of course, was to collaborate in this alchemy, a dance partner who neither led nor followed. An objective (though it rarely is) vision for the work, uncluttered by ego.

The boy has had some success and, after several abortive attempts to launch the glider, looks around for a parent to assist. Watching the scene play out, he feels only moderately saddened by the absence of his own children, is perhaps curious at the omission. In the end he had begged, sensed in that moment all the grief to come.

He wonders why Lucca. Why Pollex chose here to unravel a marriage. This Renaissance town of a hundred churches, so often besieged and occupied and sold. He wonders what fraught and terrible thoughts played out in the man's mind during those final hours.

The softest of breezes brushes across his forearm, gustless, barely anything. He pictures the jay in its nest opening up the live gecko, the skin easily penetrated, its warm, sinewy interior shared among the bird's young. He thinks of the lovers he is yet to have, whether such presumption is arrogant at this stage of life. Wonders if the protective layer around his heart is any more substantial. He would like to have come here with her, perhaps in a cooler season, climb the tower, hire a tandem and slalom along the fortress wall until the cicadas quietened and gave way to a distant aria.

Fly, Icarus, Fly

They set out, five of them, across barleyed fields, tamping down pathways like arteries, idling in the warmth of early summer. The others insisting on a convoluted route, sometimes backtracking, as if leading them to some clandestine camp, and the power that came with this. They were in his brother's year, the other three, boys with an aura of menace, who could lurch from matey to malevolent and back again in a breath. Volatile, like a gas. They swaggered like gangsters, smoked as if it was something they'd always done, the hierarchy among them today unsaid yet irrefutable, he and Blue underlings. An initiation of sorts, he supposed, prospect of entry to their number.

He understood none of the in-jokes or slick catchphrases, assumed his brother did. Violence, or a version of it, was ritualistic, regular. Punches to arms, headlocks, displays of martial arts moves that looked half-learned, mostly against each other, but then every half-mile or so these aimed at Blue, who shrugged them off like someone refusing a dance. Himself more a target of words than assaults, mockery that called into question his sexual experience, or lack of, his undeveloped body. When offered a cigarette he went to take it, his brother snatching it away, answering for him, the others laughing as Blue, to appease them, lit it himself, stifled the cough as best he could.

'Soft cunts,' the tall one said, the words to him seeming unsustainable together, like butter in a hot pan.

The others boasted of winnings from the alleyway behind the school sports hall, coins tossed to a wall, a successful trajectory coming from the wrist, as if the activity rivalled for technique sports played on the other side of the brickwork. He wondered what size their egg collections were, whether they dwarfed his brother's, if today would grant permission to view them.

At one point, where a quadrant of fields met, they discovered an adder furled beneath a sheet of corrugated iron, its dorsal patterning confusing the eye, as if it had no end or beginning. A prehistoric thing, it seemed to him, at once fascinating and unsettling, and for a moment they all stood in silence beguiled by its strange beauty. An inert creature and yet they could sense its great kinetic energy, felt it worthy of their respect. It was both vulnerable and imperious, and whereas another animal would likely have been extinguished at their hands, the sheet was merely laid gently down.

Further on, the woods spiced by pines, summer a

promise you could believe, the tall one every now and then taking his knife to bark, marking territory like a dog. Still the criss-crossing, doubling back, the promise of some great treasure, a rare species perhaps, a nest site you trusted to no one.

They arrived at the foot of a tall beech, the others pausing, announcing wordlessly that this was their destination. His brother put a hand to the bark, smoothed it like a horse's mane, and they all looked up, saw that it rose to another world.

'Just rooks up there,' Blue said. 'We came this far for that?'

'It was a matter of trust,' the tall one said. 'This first, then we'll show you something good.'

'There are no branches,' his brother said, meaning nothing to get purchase on, and one of them produced a rope from his pack and threw it at their feet, and Blue took it.

'Not you,' one of them said, 'him,' and this fear rose in him at all that height.

'Told you they're chicken shit.'

'He'll take too long,' his brother said. Said it would be boring to watch.

The rope's length was enough to loop over the lowest branch and fall back to them, his brother fashioning a slipknot, easing it upwards until tight. They could have helped, the others – offered bunk ups to give him a start

– but didn't. On his third attempt, Blue found enough height to reach over the lowest bough and heft himself up.

'If you touch him when I'm up there,' Blue called out, 'I'll fight you all when I'm down. I'll lose but so will one of you.'

And so he watched as his brother rose through the latticed cluster of limbs, bobbing and weaving like a boxer, testing potential routes in his mind before committing. Neither was he too proud to retreat a few steps, recalibrate the course as a climber would a rock face.

Blue was high enough now that the rooks got some sense of his presence, a mammal-like volume rising from morsels of chatter to bursts of serrated chiding. Wing beats starting up in applause, alarm caws issued like spitting fat.

By the time his brother was parallel to the first nests, the sky had darkened to a formless mass, bird morphing with bird, chaos and order. Still he progressed, edging out along one of the tapering boughs, hands and feet like an efficient but slow piston. Blue had told him his theory once, inherited from the badlands of home, a calculation to test the weight-bearing property of a branch. Once you could touch forefingers and thumbs around it, you went no further. It was why they build their nests that far out. A compromise. Exposed to the elements and predation from the air, but nothing without wings gets to them.

He tried to calculate the height of his brother: 40 feet, perhaps more. The rooks mobbing him now, this strange new predator inching itself amid their colony, shredding the air around his brother in furious sorties, a rhapsody of shrieks, strident and demented. This innate, mechanical response of all things, he thought, to protect their young. An ancient calling, diminishing your own worth for the sake of the species.

And still his brother there, holding his head tight to the branch, unable to risk freeing an arm in defence, waiting for a pause in the onslaught that wouldn't come. One or two rooks venturing close enough to jab and claw at flesh, like a film. The lads beside him, now grinning, entertained by the spectacle they had engineered. And himself, unable to find breath or to blink, both horrified and enthralled at Blue's exploits, this gesture undertaken in his stead.

On and on, they kept at him, the birds' programming knowing only this. And his brother docile now, the torque in him gone, but still calculating the odds, still thinking it possible. Six feet from the nearest nest now, a few more shuffles through this storm of birds, what seemed now like the entire rookery coming at him, the attack a thing of synchronicity and wonder. One egg, he thought. He is only going to take one egg, and he almost spoke it as a plea. Beside him, the others had quietened, even they in thrall of his brother's bravado, perhaps scared of it. The noise everything now, barbed and colliding with itself, no start or finish to it, the sound of life resisting death, genetically coded survival.

When the branch cracked it registered as an intrusion, a catalyst to something else. The rooks, too, sensed it, easing their intensity, perhaps knowing that a shift had occurred. And the second crack, louder yet ushering in a near silence as bird and branch and brother began their dispersal. A shower of everything from this display now falling to them, nests and tree and Blue, rooks treading air above this and the silence thickening. Every now and then a branch toyed with his brother, altered his shape, had its say in the route he took.

Blue hit the ground a dozen or so feet from them, an unnatural sound, of two things coming together that shouldn't, his shoulder folding in on itself, a flail of limbs, head claiming its own patch of ground to collapse into. A crumpling, and in that moment all humans' failed attempts to fly.

And then a stillness, save a cluster of twigs and leaves confetti-ing him, birds alighting onto branches, laying fresh claim to the tree, those with nests intact returning to them, the others ponderous then indifferent. A dozen or so broken eggs garlanding the ground around his brother, embryonic forms emerged from shells, featherless and translucent, some with small movements. Flight never known, only plummet.

And his brother, this indomitable warrior, now unmoving and silent, the air between them thick with an awfulness, and it seemed so silly that this thing had happened. This shifting of one world into another, and himself witness to this juncture, to birds dead and dying, all their evolution undone, his brother somewhere between these states.

Waves of nausea now, almost separate from him, a pulsing of their own, and his knowing there was both something he should be doing and nothing that could be done. He sensed the others running, as if in trouble and that putting distance between them and this place was an effective tactic, and for a second he thought to do the same, to flee what had built all day and had concluded in a few seconds. To be no part of it or of what would follow.

Then some instinct forcing him towards his brother, this abomination of reconfigured bones, misshapen yet intact, like something thrown there. A thing in need of fixing. He tried to recall the direction they'd come, figured they'd walked a couple of hours. The sun should be a clue, but not one he could decode. If he walked an hour, there would be something to recognise, the gulley they'd ran through, a couple of coast-bound gulls. He could not assume the others would fetch help.

Instead he sat down against the tree and hummed a tune their mother taught them as children, hoped Blue could hear it.

And his brother now a young adult, stricken within himself, how it wasn't right to keep someone like that: you would finish it off, were it an animal. Allow the thing its dignity. The law, though, clear: enough life to preserve, a carcass that with nutrients administered could continue a functioning of sorts. These early days of wires and tubes and hope alternating with despair, his parents drinking from lunchtime, though never together, more unsaid than said from now on.

When the petrification in him receded that day, he had stroked Blue's head, told him it would be alright, then he did run, picked a direction in his head and propelled himself.

It must have been two hours before his brother got to the hospital, perhaps three. His pelvis shattered, left arm and leg broken, none of which could be treated until he was stable, could be sedated. A coma induced, the bleed on his brain their focus. A man came out of the theatre, talked them through it. How the scalp was sliced and peeled back, a section of the skull cut away to relieve pressure. He found comedy in this, that they would glue the piece back at a later date, like a broken vase. The scalp then pulled back, secured to itself again.

And then they waited, watched the ventilator rise and fall, his brother this fleshly thing kept alive by pumps and prayer.

They visited twice daily to begin with, frequency diminishing as progress did. At first he saw his parents beg for the removal of danger, pledge to accept anything in return for this. Let him just survive this, they said, unknowing or uncaring of what this could mean.

Then a slowness to things, his brother in time having to learn anew, reconnect muscles with signals, or signals with muscles, he forgets which. Some small speech returning, more a noise than words, something creaturely, a thing with more vowels than it should. Finally a transition off the acute ward, returning for operations when he was able to. He can, with effort, feed himself on a good day. They even took him out for his 18th, pushed the wheelchair up to a table in a beer garden, half a pint via a straw.

And then the lexicon shifting, his brother airbrushed a little each day from the future.

You're an only-child now, his mother had said to him one saturnine evening as she watched the sea squall from her window, and he turned the phrase over in his head for days, knew it in time to be both true and false. Knew the absence would grow and grow, that his brother would become folkloric, vaporous, life defined as either pre- or post- that day, not just for Blue, for all of them. Forever an approximation of himself, this boy, now a man, who hadn't cheated death but merely borrowed something from it.

And now an adult in his thirties, but with only 15 years of living to show for that. A dilution of one half, and the knowledge of this. A boy in man's body, mind consigned to – to what? The thoughts of a child? Or worse, of mental processes that were lucid and mature, yet beyond expression. Communication reduced to a primitive exchange, a pre-language where Blue's words – so often a sequence of profanities – took minutes to form, brief windows sanctioned when fatigue and despondency receded.

Movement coming vicariously, limbs lifted to be washed, torso turned like a pig on a spit, cavities eviscerated. Weekly visits to a common room, where he would be lowered into a window-side chair, head supported by a horseshoe cushion. Spoon-fed and another form of protest as he spat food over a tireless nurse. Comatose patients, he supposed, at least had insentience going for them. It seemed unfathomably cruel that Blue should have lived every one of the days to have passed since that day in the woods.

And today's visit, he watches as his brother stares vacantly into mid-distance, perhaps registering a pigeon scull by, climbing in his mind one of the tall pines across the lawn. Could climb anything, he could.

Does he remember the fall? They said he probably doesn't, that the anchoring memory of his former life was likely moored somewhere earlier that day. A dream sequence, repeating, forever inconclusive. And his own replaying of Blue's descent, looping ceaselessly in those first months, the silence of it, the un-noise of the fall, a thing beyond comprehension.

He asks the nurses if their father had visited, more from habit than hope, knowing the man came to terms with the past by not revisiting it. He reads to his brother from the newspaper, tells him about the village he lives in along the coast. The kids ghillying for crabs off the sea wall there, as they once had.

And later, when it is just the two of them, a silent

entreaty issued from Blue's eyes, to do the right thing, and he wanted to give this finality to him, but all he could do was hold his brother and promise not to let go.

Upgrade

There were no more jobs for life; he'd been told as much.

'We don't owe you a living, Roland,' the woman half his age had said. 'There'll be a fair package and with outstanding leave you can finish Friday.'

'Could I still come in some days?' he asked. 'You wouldn't have to pay me.'

He was given a brass carriage clock and a blended whisky, the presentation of which spanned the last five minutes of the working week. Colin, Bex the new girl and Jeremy were there, but everyone else was in a meeting, which he knew was code for at the pub. I should make a speech, he thought, but by the time he conceived of anything to say, the room was empty. He placed the accoutrements of 35 years into a plastic box, coughed his nervous cough and slunk home to see how life played itself out.

Tens of accounts jobs were applied for, a few of which yielded interviews, but the other candidates were invariably in their twenties or thirties, devoid of the doleful expression that now greeted Roland in the mirror each morning. *The company's looking for fresh ideas*, came the euphemistic feedback. *Your maturity would be wasted here.*

Walking home he had to concede that indeed he didn't have any ideas, fresh or otherwise. Instead he told himself that he had his health, which was something to be grateful for.

'You'll have to retrain,' his wife said that evening. 'I'm not doing extra hours just because you're useless.'

Such castigation had become frequent since she'd started an evening class titled 'Elementary Magic'. Stefan, the course's facilitator, who'd self-published three volumes of his methods, used magic to 'help you transform your life'.

'It's all about asking the universe for what you want,' Greta said. 'About unlocking the power within. I'd take you along were you not such an embarrassment.'

'Abracadabra,' he said under his breath.

Where possible Roland maintained routine. The alarm still shrilled at seven-fifteen, whereupon he would shower and shave before preparing their porridge or scrambled eggs on granary toast, although his wife was increasingly stocking the cupboards with food he couldn't pronounce: quinoa, açai, kimchi, baobab. He wasn't even sure it *was* food. In the end they agreed on separate cupboards, separate mealtimes.

Once Greta left for the real world each day, he kept the mornings full with the list of housework she'd left him, the undertaking of which he found surprisingly gratifying. The afternoons, though, were interminable and harder to fill. He tried building a replica of the *Mayflower* that would apparently fit in a bottle, but the slight tremor in his right hand he'd hidden so well from occupational health, rendered the activity impossible. Collecting stamps made him feel older than his 54 years and the garden had always been Greta's preserve.

'You can mow the lawn but leave the flora – you'll only ruin it,' which in truth was somewhat of a fantasy of his these days. Just to see her face.

Other pastimes were explored, though with little success. His homemade beer wasn't fit for the homeless – smelling faintly of kerosene and tasting little better, and the guitar, he discovered, required more patience and longer, less stubbier fingers than he possessed.

Meanwhile the vacancies pages seemed to diminish each week, and as the months since his last employment grew, so the interviews dried up. He began applying for all manner of work: security guard, chauffeur, driving the children's train at the model village – but it seemed the world could manage quite happily without his talents. His redundancy package, he calculated, would last another eleven weeks, at which point he would have to suffer the indignity of asking his wife to buy the four cans of Boddington's that, on finishing the blended whisky, had become his evening ritual. Perhaps he should buy one of the super strength lagers, which offered a greater ABV-to-cost ratio, albeit at the expense of quantity. Greta used to indulge in a little gin, which would be better than nothing, but even that had become victim of her new regime.

'Stefan says alcohol dampens the fire within us,' she said.

He needed to think more laterally, like the guy he'd read about who had a foolproof system for the horses, though obviously you had to send him an initial investment, and surely if it was so prosperous, why did the guy need to share it?

Later at dinner his wife scowled across the table.

'Something'll turn up,' he said wistfully.

'Where's the man I married?' she spat.

He tried to remember, but the images appeared grainy, as if those days had been incorrectly archived, or had happened to someone else. Perhaps they should have had children, adopted once their own had been ruled out. They would come home to visit every now and then in the holidays, bring their own children.

In an attempt to ward off loneliness, Roland found himself filling the days with superfluous appointments.

'Take one each morning with food,' said his GP, handing him the prescription. He never took the pills; it was just nice to visit someone regularly – sort of a trivial case of Munchausen, he supposed. In the waiting room one week he picked up a leaflet for an ME support group, which he attended for a while, taking advantage of the tea and cake on offer. He never quite understood how talking about their illness helped them, yet he was sorry to leave when Janet, the group's founder and ME veteran of twenty-two years, learned he was only a little bit tired, and even then only for around half an hour or so mid-afternoon, whereupon he would take a nap. Walking home it annoyed him, how people were so precious about their clubs, how you had to be this or that to join them. He should start his own, a group for redundant men whose wives ate non-food and were into magic. They would meet at his house every Tuesday afternoon, eat cake, drink tea and then go home for naps.

In the meantime, after his domestic duties each day, Roland took to short circuitous walks through the sub-urban streets with their manicured gardens, striding purposefully as if his destination wasn't merely his own home. His now-empty tan briefcase accompanied him as a prop, giving, he hoped, the façade of respectability. Neighbours were greeted by his affected smile, but it was obvious they could smell his failure, giving him a wide berth lest it proved infectious. Their pity bore into him as he walked past: *Washed up at that age, such a shame.* The less brutish ones would sometimes engage him: *Did he want to join their book group? Perhaps he could take the minutes at the next neighbourhood watch meeting.* All very tempting, but he knew a thing or two about 'groups' now, and would not be rushing to join any more just yet.

As the weeks passed, despondency thick as treacle fell upon him, helped in no part by having to cut his Boddington's intake to two cans per night. Grooming was soon neglected; seemed it was mostly for other people's benefit anyway. Everyone should grow a full beard once in their life, he thought, although his own proved to be a rather patchy affair. Pyjamas and a dressing gown served well unless he left the house, which he rarely did now. He wondered if reading might not be something he'd enjoy, but the shelves were increasingly full of Greta's New Age tripe, endless spines of pulp on the occult, crystals, mysticism and witchcraft – written, no doubt, by Stefan and his kind. The library was an option, but gazing in the window one time he saw that ME Janet worked there – presumably when she wasn't tired – and the thought of asking her what books she recommended terrified him.

Roland's marriage – unspectacular but until now functional – drifted aimlessly as if routine had been its anchor, Greta withdrawing herself from him a little more each day, first verbally, which suited him, then physically, which he couldn't work out whether it suited him or not.

'I can't think about all that when there's this financial worry,' she said. 'And besides, look at the state of you.'

This coming from someone with a wart the size of a garden pea on her nose. How had he put up with it all these years? In fact he was certain it had grown of late, with one or two additional hairs sprouting proudly.

Perhaps his mood *would* be improved by a little how's-your-father, yet the prospect of such seemed as unlikely as it had ever been. Returning early from work one day, Greta caught him masturbating into her Kays catalogue, which in a way he was grateful for, the activity a rather desultory, tiresome affair, one he could anticipate no end to.

'At your age!' she said, banishing him to the spare room, where he found the abandoned *Mayflower* and a life-sized cardboard cut-out of Stefan, beneath which the words AWAKEN THE MAGIC IN YOU appeared.

Each night that week, as she went to bed, his wife kicked the door, cursing and muttering, cackling almost.

'Things are going to change, Roland, just you wait!'

The pain, when it came, seemed to manifest somewhere deep in his marrow, as if the very core of him was sick. Coupled with this was an exhaustion the like of which he'd not known, the sort of lethargy that made flu seem a triviality. The sort of tiredness ME Janet spoke of.

'A nasty bug,' the doctor Greta eventually agreed to call out said. 'Lots of funny things going around. Keep the fluids up, right as rain in no time.'

But no time came and went. As did lots of time.

By now a single trip to the bathroom took a steady hour of building up to, the resulting fatigue rendering him bedridden until the next call of nature arrived. He'd assumed his wife's antipathy for him would rise another notch or two, but if anything her voice mellowed, her little digs receding to nothing. She started to fetch him his meals on a tray, real food, porridge and cake and endless cups of tea, which he rather felt he deserved at the moment. After his dinner she'd even bring up an open can of Boddington's, and when he asked for a second, to help the aches, she tutted but in a friendly way.

'Got to keep the fluids up, I guess,' she said.

And if it wasn't for feeling utterly lousy, he wondered if he hadn't found his ideal lifestyle after all. Perhaps, when he started to get better, he wouldn't tell people. No point rushing these things, better to make sure.

The doorbell brought him out of a fitful sleep, one which had featured Stefan showing him pictures of ME Janet in a Kays catalogue, except on closer examination he saw that the model was actually Greta, not as she was now but when he first met her, which he supposed was rather beautiful. Come to think of it, she was looking a lot younger these days. The doorbell might have been part of the dream sequence had there not followed three evenly-spaced knocks. It was perfectly reasonable to ignore it, he said to himself, his energy levels at an all-time low, and yet each time he thought the caller had given up, the bell would sound again, followed by three more knocks.

It must have taken him several minutes to negotiate

the stairs, but he could see the silhouette of person or persons through the frosted glass. Assuming it was someone recruiting membership for a group, he called out that he wasn't interested, that he was going to start his own.

'Delivery for Greta,' came back the reply. 'Needs a signature.' And so reluctantly Roland opened the door.

It took both of the well-built delivery men to lift the box from the back of the van and heft it up the garden path. After he signed on his wife's behalf, the men left it upright in the hallway, sniggering to each other when he asked what it was.

'An upgrade,' one of them shouted from the gate.

Another Stefan cut-out, he thought. A month ago he might have opened it, when curiosity was still something he was capable of, but in truth he felt like death. No, not like death, because death surely felt better than this. And so he started up the stairs, when a noise, barely audible, came from the box. There it was again. He must have imagined it, though, because for all the world it sounded like a cough.

Fireflies

The copper-coloured sky of an hour ago has darkened, although there is still enough light to walk by. From the tall trees inland you hear an exodus of rooks, wings clattering upwards in applause. You call to your son, who lags behind, this annual pilgrimage along the coast path, the emotion of the thing, taking its toll.

So many hours of your own adolescence spent along this path and you strain to hear the sounds of youth: the purr of your reel once cast, the sonorous slop of weights striking distant water, the rhythmic *tick tick* as you wound in the slack.

'Is it much further?' he says. You've promised him a shandy at the pub.

Earlier, after placing the flowers down, you stopped to watch a cormorant skim above the water, tight to the surf, its elongated neck cleaving the air like an arrow shaft. You hoped for a kestrel, hovering at eye level, out over the cliff edge, but there've been none. She always spotted birds first, when the two – and later three – of you walked this path, her keen eye filtering out all irrelevance, a distant silhouette identified before its presence was even known to you. Watching your son you wonder how much of this she passed down, what her legacy will be.

You look out beyond the headland, picture the rusting hulks of wrecked ships that ghost the sea floor, forests of kelp slowly claiming them. The wind is gusting now, blinding you if you look into it, the air sharp, briny. Herring gulls and fulmars ride the thermals in long, graceful arcs, the easy rhythm of their flight soothing you a little. The gulls on the beach below issue proud, barbarous cries as they delve into the seaweed or jab at stranded cuttlefish. Beyond them, groups of sanderlings gather on the tideline in search of sand shrimps, their forms scuttling comically back and forth with each breaking wave, froths of foam eddying around them.

A year on and you still wonder what kind of a life can be fashioned in her absence.

You look out to the open water, its irregular surface specked with half a dozen fishing boats. A tanker sits sombrely on the horizon. For a moment you think you see the dorsal fin of a basking shark cutting through the swell a few hundred yards out, but by the time you find the spot with the binoculars, it has gone. Most, if not all of them, will have left for the warmer waters of the south by now. On the tip of the promontory ahead, sea heaves at rock, slamming into coves, the water forced up a blowhole with each wave, spuming into the wind.

As dusk draws in you climb a steep section of the path, sit on the tip of a headland looking out to sea and wait for him to catch up. A fishing boat flanks the coast, its silhouette crimping the water's surface, the chunter of its engine pulsing faintly up to you both. Behind, in the vessel's wake, the sea gleams a luminous azure, as phosphorescent algae are ignited by the turbulence, giving the boat a shimmering tail as if a million fireflies were following it.

You watch your son blow into his hands, steel yourself for the year he won't want or need to come on this walk, his own life taking over, the memory of her receding a little more. You wonder if you'll be strong enough on your own.

Inland the last of the day's light washes over the fields. Ahead you can just make out the bone-white walls of the pub along the coast.

Your arm around his shoulder, you want to ask: Am I enough?

'Race you there,' you say instead.

Acknowledgements

Fiction is never the endeavour of one person alone,[1] and I'd like to offer heartfelt thanks to the following people, whose inimitable presence in my life helped shape the book you are holding. They say the greatest gift a writer can receive from his or her parents is a dysfunctional childhood, and I would like to express particular gratitude to Les and Sandra on this account. Certainly the bouts of moderate violence and enduring disdain they held for one another would weave its way into any number of characters and set-pieces. And imagine how that scene in 'Confessions of a Loss Adjuster' would have turned out had my father not arrived home from work unexpectedly that day in 1993, to find my mother in close liaison with Craig from HR. Further, although unclear which set of chromosomes bestowed on me the mild asthma that led to my non-attendance at school for much of the winter term, I am grateful for the introversion, and as a result the bookishness, this resulted in. Particular mention must also

---

1 Except that it kind of is.

be made of Mr *******,[1] my erstwhile secondary school teacher, who in his own delightfully abusive way ran the after-school ornithological society, which although not explicitly prohibiting female members, never seemed to acquire any. Although not strictly biographical, the teacher in 'Raven Mad' drew heavily on those endless evenings in the bird hide at Cley Marshes, warmed only as we were by the steady furnishing of brandy. Lastly, credit must go to Mrs Artherton,[2] who as a bored suburban housewife seduced my best friend, Richard Hester,[3] after we had cleaned her husband's car in the school holidays. Their summer-long tryst, as well as underwriting much of our business's modest income that year (and ensuring Mr Artherton's car was the cleanest this side of Fakenham), had me spending short but frequent periods in the Arthertons' boutique library.

---

1 Name redacted for fear of libel suit, though boys in Years 1 through 4 will know who I mean.

2 Real name used, as the Arthertons later moved to Canada, where this book will likely not be published.

3 Ditto. He's probably still dining out on the anecdote.

Supporters

Unbound is a new kind of publishing house. Our books are funded directly by readers. This was a very popular idea during the late eighteenth and early nineteenth centuries. Now we have revived it for the internet age. It allows authors to write the books they really want to write and readers to support the books they would most like to see published.

The names listed below are of readers who have pledged their support and made this book happen. If you'd like to join them, visit www.unbound.com.

A.Q.S.
Paul Allen
Colin Appleton
Jon Appleton
Mark Appleton
A. J. Ashworth
Tim Atkinson
Sharon Bakar
Claire Baldwin
Richard Baxter

Alexander Bell
Douglas Bence
Laura Besley
Susmita Bhattacharya
Nigel Blandford
Richard Blandford
David John Bonnett
Margaret Bonnett
Nicholas Bonnett
Carys Bray

Moira Briggs
Charlie Brotherstone
Kate Brown
Victoria Brown
Anthony Caleshu
Aifric Campbell
Charlie Campbell
Neil Campbell
Clare Carlin
Liz Carr

Adelia Chamberlain
Elaine Chiew
Martyn Clayton
Cleopatra Loves Books
Sylvia Cohen
Clodagh O Connor
Isabel Costello
Ruby Cowling
Ailsa Cox
Dan Coxon
Michelle Coyne
Kaori Crawford
Martyn Crocker
Emma Crosley
Jane Damesick
Miriam Darlington
Rupert Dastur
Paul Bassett Davies
Katie Davis
Holly Dawson
Rachael de Moravia
Emily Devane
Deborah Dooley
Lucy Durneen
Kathryn Eastman
Jamie Edgecombe
Ken Elkes
Mary & Tim Fowler
Sarah Franklin
Caron Freeborn
Nick French
Eileen Furby
Hayden Gabriel
Patrick Gale
Sarah Ganczarski
Frances Gapper

Vanessa Gebbie
Sarah Geraghty
Martha Gifford
Lisa Glass
Rhoda Greaves
Michelle Green
Tracey Guiry
Suzan Gunnee
Cat Hamilton
Linda Hancox
Liam Harkin
Andrea Harman
Jack Harris
Alan Harvey
Francoise Harvey
Lander Hawes
Lauren Hayhurst
Tania Hershman
Ian Hobbs
Peter Hobbs
Ian Hocking
James Hodgson
Jon Hotten
Emma-Jane Hughes
Naomi Johnson
Friðrik Sólnes Jónsson
Rae Joyce
Elena Kaufman
Zarabéa Kayani
Luke Kennard
Louise Kennedy
Mele Kent
Dan Kieran
Martin G. King
Lania Knight
Pierre L'Allier

Charles Lambert
Chris Lambert
Zoe Lambert
Nick Lord Lancaster
Anne Landricombe
    and Christine Gill
John Lavin
Jason Le Masurier
Michelle Le Masurier
Jonathan Lee
Toby Litt
Frieda Little
Alison Lock
Rowena Macdonald
Adnan Mahmutovic
Joanne Martin
John Martin
Riona McCormack
Anthony McGowan
Ian McGuire
Danielle McLaughlin
Catherine McNamara
Wendy McQueen
Joe Melia
Erinna Mettler
Mark Middleton
Alban Miles
Annika Milisic-
    Stanley
Elizabeth Miller
James Miller
John Mitchinson
Lucy Moffatt
Alison Moore
Steve Moran
Graham Mort

Ruth Nassar
Carlo Navato
Annemarie Neary
Felicia Negomireanu
Andrew Neilson
Marios Nicolaou
Nuala O'Connor
Valerie O'Riordan
Marella Oppenheim
Jeremy Osborne
Scott Pack
Lev Parikian
Hilary Payne
Emma Pearce
Sylvia Petter
Jonathan Pinnock
Justin Pollard
John Pollex
Dan Powell
Alex Preston
Jessica Priestley
Laura Quigley
Alexa Radcliffe-Hart
Uma Rajasingam
Kelly Reynolds
Katy Rink

Riptide Journal
Laura Ritchie
Jane Roberts
Imogen Robertson
HJ Rose-Innes
Eimear Ryan
Amanda Saint
Danny Scheinmann
David Sergeant
Benjamin Serpell
Margaret Shambrook
Babs Short
Valerie Sirr
Philip Slattery
Angela K. Smith
Martin Smith
Richard Smyth
Ruby Speechley
Christopher Stanley
Lisa Stewart
Rachel Stirling
Tabatha Stirling
Ashley Stokes
Anne Summerfield
Alicja Syska
Sam Talbot

Justine Taylor
William Telford
Terri Writes
Margaret Thomas
Mike Scott Thomson
Laura Tickle
Paul Tomlin
Simon Travers
Rachel Trezise
Chloe Turner
Sherri Turner
Lee Upton
Neil Vogler
Felton Vowler
Julie Vowler
Jim Walkley-Cox
Lindsay Waller-
    Wilkinson
Jayne White
Joel Willans
Kate Wilson
Simon Withers
Michelle Witney
Stella Wulf
Veronica